Logan backed away, circling. Woman or not, Stella Raines could be lethal. A specialist in martial arts, she had been TEC's chief instructor in hand-to-hand confrontation since she was recruited from Interpol in 2005. Every graduate of the TEC Academy, men and women alike, had been taught by Stella Raines. And it was the secret dread of all of them that they might one day have to face someone like Stella in real combat.

Logan was seeing the reality of that now, as the woman bored in for another attack. She had no recollection of him, of course, but now he saw that even the TEC uniform he wore meant nothing to her. A blur of punishing fists and feet confronted him, staggering him again, and Logan realized that Stella wasn't playing games here. She was a time jumper. He had interfered with her, and she meant to kill him . . .

By Dan Parkinson
Published by Ballantine Books:

The Gates of Time:
THE WHISPERS
FACES OF INFINITY

Timecop
VIPER'S SPAWN
THE SCAVENGER
BLOOD TIES

TIMECOP

Blood Ties

Dan Parkinson

Based on the Universal Television Series
created for Television by Mark Verheiden

Based on the characters created by
Mike Richardson & Mark Verheiden

A Del Rey® Book
THE BALLANTINE PUBLISHING GROUP • NEW YORK

A Del Rey® Book
Published by The Ballantine Publishing Group
Copyright © 1999 by Universal Studios Publishing Rights, a Division of Universal Studios Licensing, Inc. All rights reserved.

www.randomhouse.com/BB/

Library of Congress Catalog Card Number: 98-093428

ISBN 0-345-42197-3

Manufactured in the United States of America

First Ballantine Books Edition: April 1999

10 9 8 7 6 5 4 3 2 1

TIMECOP

Blood Ties

Prologue

New York City
1929

Harry Sheffield's long fingers danced through the lingering final trills of "Bye, Bye, Blackbird," holding that last, minor chord as its little echoes faded away into the muted murmur of voices here and there around the room. The piano in the Phoenix Club was no match for the fine, lacquered grand he had played two years before in his virtuoso performance with the Boston Symphony Orchestra, but it was a good Wurlitzer and its tones rang bell-true here on the recessed, brass-and-velvet bandstand of the Phoenix Club.

Not that anybody besides himself really cared. A virtuoso pianist becomes simply a piano player the moment he steps away from his art and accepts a six-nights-a-week contract to entertain the diners. For Harry Sheffield, that moment had come at the age of twenty-one. Without a doting family or a wealthy patron, art is the short road to starvation.

So Harry had packed away his dreams of composing the

greatest of concertos, and now he pounded the keys for Rudy Valentine at thirty dollars a week.

The silence brought a smattering of reluctant applause, and he noticed again that there was something different about the mood of the Phoenix tonight. Early on, it had been the usual crowd—a few drunks and hecklers at the front tables, a bar mitzvah party in the alcove, some on-the-towners playing at the easy life, a gaggle of opera-goers fresh from the Black Orchid, and a larger crowd from the Orpheum where "Broadway Melody" shared the marquee with Mickey Mouse.

But now the casuals had drifted away, and there was a different bunch. The air was nervous with tension, sub-dued with expectant dread. Busboys had cleared away the front tables, and those diners who remained weren't din-ing. They were just waiting—sad-eyed Italian faces and lumpy overcoats along one side, the McGintys along the other.

There had been a rumor on the streets, that a deal would be made between the Spirelli family and Seamus McGinty for control of rackets on the Lower East Side. But nobody knew whether the deal would involve money or blood.

Harry ran a few riffs along the upper register, eased into bass chords, and glanced at the little cellar trap half-hidden by the piano. Something nervous was happening here tonight.

He launched into "Crazy Rhythm" for sixteen bars, then downchorded expertly and blended in a touch of "Desert Song," and nobody seemed to notice. He realized that it didn't matter what he played, as long as he kept playing. Nobody was listening to the music. They would listen only if he quit.

Harry Sheffield was used to being lonely. It was a way of life for him, and he had about given up on any miracles coming along to change that. But the young pianist felt lonelier than usual tonight, alone on that lighted bandstand while out in the shadowy clubroom men with $200 suits and hidden guns glared at one another across an empty dance floor.

He noticed then that the waiters and busboys had all disappeared. Something was happening here.

Maybe it was because of the bandstand rise that Harry saw what no one else in the place seemed to see—a sudden swirling, coalescing shift of reality in the little corridor leading to the kitchen. For an instant, in that little space, existence seemed to spin, whirl, and collapse inward upon itself. An instant only, then there was a man there, suspended three feet above the floor. In the instant Harry saw him he dropped to the floor, crouching, then ducked behind a velvet drape.

"Desert Song" became the overture from "Die Walkürie," and Harry didn't even notice it.

Across the club, the big oaken door opened and three McGintys edged in, two with their hands under the coats and one—Seamus himself—carrying a leather satchel.

All hell seemed to break loose at that moment. The strange man from the kitchen corridor appeared at a booth alcove, holding a lethal-looking something with a red light on top of it. He lunged and pivoted, grabbed the valise from Seamus McGinty, and whirled around. The other two McGintys went down as though they had been poleaxed, and the man with the odd weapon sprinted three steps toward the kitchen, then doubled over the outstretched foot of a small, dark-haired woman whose sable wrap was thrown aside to expose a large, semiautomatic handgun with an elaborate red-light beamer of its own.

"Drop and spread 'em, Bozo!" she ordered. "You're under arrest!"

Across the room, a man in some kind of uniform stepped out from between rubber plants, swinging a red-light gun this way and that. "Everybody just stay calm," he ordered. "It's TEC business."

For an instant, the scene was a frozen tableau . . . followed by chaos. It might have been Seamus McGinty who opened the ball, or it might have been Vicente Spirelli. But suddenly there were guns everywhere, and everybody was shooting at everybody else. Harry Sheffield dived behind the piano.

The roar of gunfire in the Phoenix Club was deafening. It ebbed slightly, and Harry peeked out to see bodies sprawled everywhere. Some were moving and some weren't. The girl with the sable wrap was crawling toward the bandstand, leaving a little trail of blood behind her. On impulse, the musician broke from cover just as someone kicked the girl viciously and stood over her, leveling a gun. It was Bozo, the man who had first materialized in the kitchen corridor.

With a cry Harry sprinted two steps, launched himself, and smashed into the man, who didn't see him coming. Bozo fell, dropping his gun. Harry followed, almost blind with rage. The man had assaulted a helpless, injured woman. Remembering that vicious kick, Harry swung a roundhouse blow that smashed into Bozo's face, then hit him again, as hard as he could. The man went limp, and Harry turned to the girl and picked her up. Gunfire erupted again, and he ducked and ran, back to the cover of the piano.

She was almost unconscious, bleeding from a head wound, but even through the blood and the stink of gunpowder Harry realized that never in his life had he seen anyone so beautiful. He raised the trap, eased her down through it, and crawled in after her. Beneath, the crawlway was a service ledge dropping to a small cellar.

Above them, muffled now, a few more gunshots echoed; then there was silence. In the cellar gloom she looked up at him with dazed, unfocused dark eyes. "Help me," she whispered.

"I'm trying to, miss," Harry said.

"Where's Cole?" she slurred, struggling for consciousness. "My partner . . . and the jumper . . . where are they?"

Harry eased the trap open, peering out. The Phoenix reeked of gunsmoke and silence. There were bloody bodies everywhere. Raising his head, he saw the man he had hit, sprawled now across a table with part of his head missing. Across the room, beyond fallen Spirellis and McGintys, the man with the red-light gun lay half-upright against a velvet-draped wall. He was dead. Everybody was dead.

Just beneath him, the girl's slurred voice sounded frantic. "The anomalies! Gather up the anomalies!"

"The what?"

"The . . . things that don't belong in this time," she managed. "Please . . ."

Harry crawled from the trap, skirted the piano, and made the rounds, stepping over dead gangsters. He found three of the odd-looking red-light guns, a thing like a padlock with a radio dial, and a strange bracelet strapped to the dead uniformed man's wrist.

He gathered these and returned to the trap, closing the lid just as the club's front doors burst open to the sounds of shouts and stern voices.

In the little cellar off the stage crawlway, the injured girl tied a sort of tape around all the things Harry had collected, and added a bracelet of her own. She pulled away from Harry, feeble fingers trying to manipulate the decoration on one of the bracelets.

"Here, miss." He took the bundle from her gently. "Let me help you with that. What are you trying to do with—"

"No! . . ." she breathed, and passed out.

Harry got a grip on the bracelet's raised center, tugged at it and twisted, and suddenly everything around him began to whirl crazily. By reflex he cast the bundle away from him, then watched in wide-eyed awe as the strange things disappeared in a swirling, coalescing instant of indescribable confusion.

Shouts and footfalls sounded overhead, and Harry knew it was only moments until somebody noticed the floor trap behind the piano. In the gloom of the tiny cellar he scooped the injured girl up in his arms and ducked around boilers, through pipe tunnels, and into a plumbing shaft.

He didn't know what had happened in the Phoenix Club, or who was up there now, or what would happen next. But a helpless, bleeding girl with big, dark eyes had asked him to help her, and suddenly there was nothing more important in Harry Sheffield's world than to do what he could for her.

She needed him. Harry couldn't remember anybody ever needing him before.

* * *

In the dingy little walk-up that was Harry's home, he cleaned and wrapped her wound—a short, bleeding scar just above the left temple. Sensitive fingers told him her skull was sound, but the concussion was precarious. He wrapped her in blankets and held her close as waves of delayed shock racked her.

Doc Walker came from down the street, examined her, and shrugged. "Anybody's guess," he said. "I think we can rule out paralysis or blindness. She exhibits no severe damage. But concussion is a tricky thing. Whatever you're doing, just keep doing it, Harry."

When Doc was gone, Harry covered the girl with blankets and sat by her side while she slept. When delirium set in, and nothing else would calm her, he played for her—his skill drawing Mozart's genius from the old Baldwin upright that was his only real possession.

In those hours he played as though his life depended on it, and for the first time in his life he felt that it truly did. Sometime along there, at the old Baldwin, he found himself playing things that he hadn't played before, things that nobody had played. He was making them up as he went along.

For three days he nursed the young woman, attended her, and poured out his music for her, alone in the shabby little room. His world had a focus now, he found, and that focus had dark hair and big, dark eyes.

Like an injured, helpless child she had come into his dreary life and filled it with song. And she needed him.

When her fevers became normal sleep, he slipped out for food. He heard the talk on the streets and bought a *New York Times*. There had been a shootout between two mobs at the Phoenix Club. Most of the dead were identified, among them Vicente Spirelli and Seamus McGinty. Eleven hoodlums and two other unidentified males were dead, a satchel full of money was found, but no witnesses came forward to explain what had happened.

The girl lapsed in and out of sleep, sometimes muttering and tossing, sometimes delirious, sometimes almost comatose. But on the morning of the fourth day she awoke and looked around. "You saved my life, didn't you?" she whispered, trying to recover her voice. "You're the music I clung to."

"I'm Harry," he told her. "Harry Sheffield. You were hurt, miss. I brought you here. Is there anyone I can contact for you?"

She gazed at him with eyes like dark pools, then shook her head. "No," she said. "There's no one, I guess."

"You—you can stay here," he stammered. "I mean, if you want to. I don't mind, I'd—I'd like for you to stay . . . with me."

She smiled slightly. "I know that, Harry. Your music told me." The smile collapsed as memories flooded in. "I sort of know what happened. I remember, a little . . . My God! What a mess! Cole? Is Cole? . . ."

"Your friend? I'm sorry, miss. There was so much shooting. Your friend is dead. So is Mr. Bozo. Everybody's dead. I gathered up all the—the anomaly things you wanted, but—they all disappeared. I'm sorry."

"Then I'm stuck here," she said after a while. "I can't go back. But maybe that's best. We botched it so . . . maybe there isn't even anything to go back to."

She sounded so melancholy that Harry took her hand. "If there's someplace you need to go, I'll help you get there if I can."

"No. Oh, God! We left such tracks, everything must be different now. I just have to accept that. I guess I'm not going anywhere." The smile returned, tentative and wistful. "Hi, Harry Sheffield. I'm Kaki."

Lower Manhattan Island
June 27, 1776

On this night the sky was as high as a tall man's head. It glowed bloody red amidst its smokes, and the fitful vapors reeked of filth and burning hovels. In this hellish vale of flames and swirling darkness, redcoat soldiers slogged through muddy streets, their bayonets affixed. Their blades dripped with the blood of saboteurs and innocent bystanders alike, while wretches in rags fled before them.

Fire was everywhere, in this village above the East River. Sheds, shacks, and tents flared and blazed as drifting embers spread from the better buildings. Squalid clusters of cottages joined sturdy hostels in the inferno, blazes unchecked as the troops of General Sir William Howe went about their bloody work.

The commander in chief of the British army in America had ordered New York secured for the arrival of his brother, Vice Admiral Lord Richard Howe, with the White Fleet of expedition. By first light of morning, it would be.

The fires of the village seemed reflected just offshore, where a flaming galley drifted on the sluggish tide, watched over by a pair of Union Jack brigs as it burned itself down to the waterline. *Heron*'s foredeck had exploded an hour before, its magazines erupting into a ball of flame that climbed upward through the mists of evening.

The work of colonial saboteurs, some said—retaliation against the quartermaster, Captain Reginald Greaves. Others, though, spoke of darker deeds and whispered of a raid by the colonial rebels who called themselves patriots. *Heron*, they said, had put in just that day, under close watch. Scuttlebutt had it that the ship carried coin taken from pirates at Rhode Island, but of course it was folly to pay heed to tavern gossip in port towns.

The firing of the galley, though, had set off tonight's business, and General Howe grasped the opportunity to make a sweep of it. Methodically, his troops worked their way up from the battery shores and down from Blount's, rousting and burning as they went.

Musket volleys and random shots echoed here and there amidst the cries of the scurrying, fleeing colonials.

In a shadowed way just off the horse pens, a man with a tar hat hid in the darkness of a shattered slope-cellar, peering through cracks as a platoon of regulars streamed past, trotting to the count of their sergeant. When they were gone, Tom Jenkins raised his head to peer about. Behind him rose the back wall of Finn's tavern, and ahead, down the strewn slope, the lapping dark waters of the East River. Out on that water sat anchored vessels—a seventy-four-gun ship of the line and its escorts. Beyond were the mud-flats of Wale Bogt, and farther out the reeking hulks of prison ships.

Jenkins was the last of his lot. There had been six of them, at evening light, but now two were dead and three captured, and he knew he would not see them again. In a moment of relative calm he crept out of the cellar, hoisted the heavy sack to his shoulder with an effort, and the sealed copper sea chest with its rope sling. Then he slipped away, into the warrens and alleys of the boatyards where darkness still prevailed over the glow of flames.

He had in mind to make his way to the north, to the woodlands beyond the fish docks, and maybe there find a skiff or pole raft that might carry him up to Hell Gate. But beyond the boatyards, sentries were everywhere and fresh troops were on the move. Even as he emerged from the rail gates, lanterns were closing in on him. If they caught him now, he'd live out his days on a prison ship. A bloody, stinking prison ship . . .

With an oath, Jenkins bolted—across a muddy cartage way and into the mouth of an alley. He heard shouts behind him and knew he had been seen. Desperately, he scuttled through the narrow passage and out the other end, only to turn and dive back into the darkness as redcoats marched into view there, carrying lanterns.

A midden path between shacks gave him momentary cover until flames burst from a roof nearby and flooded the alleyway with ruddy light. Bent beneath the weight of his burdens, Jenkins broke from the midden path and ran for darker shadows across the alley. There were shouts. He felt a stunning, sickening pain as a musket barked behind him, then his left leg went limp. He fell against a rough wall, staggered for a moment, and went on, his free hand clawing at the wall to support him. At the next turn he lost his balance and fell, but still he struggled onward, crawling, pulling the heavy sack and the sea chest behind him.

In a tiny kitchen yard behind a shuttered shack he found

a cistern and struggled half-upright, clinging to its lip. He felt weak and dizzy. With a heave that almost made him pass out, he hoisted the sack to the well's edge and pushed it over. The thunder of musketry somewhere near hid its sound as it splashed into the dark water below.

Panting, he removed the copper sea chest from its slings and sent it after the sack. As it disappeared into the well he sagged there, weak and shaking.

"Liberty," Jenkins whispered. "And damn King George to hell."

Tom Jenkins, carpenter and American patriot, made it another seventy yards that night before becoming one of the nameless casualties of the occupation of New York by British expeditionary forces. He went as far as he could go, then struggled upright, clinging to the rungs of a tannery ladder. He died standing, facing his enemy, and never felt the heavy ball that ripped through his chest and splattered gore across the wall beyond.

There was one besides the soldiers who saw him die. From a cable loft above the boatyards, this one saw it all, and when the soldiers had gone on, she crept from the loft down the ladder to the muddy ground, gathered her skirts about her, and ran, back the way Jenkins had come.

At the humble cistern where the fugitive had left his burdens, a man in gray twenty-first-century garb was bending over the lip of the hole, attaching a miniature spectroanalyzer to a cable winch. He had been dredging, and the evidence lay beside him—a small copper-sheathed chest and a motley pile of wet debris.

She approached quietly, and from the folds of her skirt she drew a weapon not like anything ever seen in this time—or for centuries to come. "Don't move," she ordered. He froze where he stood, then turned slowly.

"You should be ashamed of yourself, George," the girl said. "Dipping into time's till? A TEC theorist should know better!"

"I'm not hurting anybody," the man said. "This wasn't found for nearly two centuries. The rest of it never was. It's a victimless crime."

"You're breaking the rules," she said coldly. "George Blake, I place you under arrest on general TEC warrant. Now just—"

In panic, the man dropped to one knee and whipped out a gun. Before he could fire it, a sizzle of searing energy pierced him and he crumpled. Behind him, beyond the cistern, shadows moved and a man stepped forward, putting away his blaster.

"Sloppy," he said critically. "Very sloppy, Boyer. Next time, watch your man's eyes, not his hands. However, you did make the arrest. You can—"

"You didn't have to kill him, Cole!" the girl snapped.

"I didn't kill him. He's only stunned. Review your texts, Boyer. A kill blast doesn't sizzle, it sings! Now let's get out of here."

While the senior timecop gathered up all traces of their presence, TEC Agent Mary Katherine Boyer dropped the copper chest back into the cistern and spent a few minutes gathering debris—bits of stone and broken brick—and dumping it in the hole. Then she marked the location carefully in her mind, using as references the new flagstaff on battery point and the ridge above the horse pens.

When Senior Agent Cole was satisfied, he attached a come-along to the unconscious prisoner. "It's your collar,

Boyer," he told the young cop. "Not bad for your first mission. Now take us home."

She snapped a short tether to her partner's sleeve, gripped the prisoner's come-along, and touched a device attached to her left wrist. Where they stood, reality seemed to swirl and coalesce, dimensions falling in upon themselves.

Then they were gone, without a trace. It was as though no one had ever been there.

TEC Headquarters
Washington, D.C.
March 9, 2008

E-warp picked up the anachronism and displayed it on the Dome of History—the big, overhead screen that was the eyes and ears of the Time Enforcement Commission. In the Dome, slowly swirling patterns of intricate color and shape—the visible representations of the timestream—were disrupted by a widening, intruding subpattern as a change in history occurred and grew, weaving itself into the fabric of downstream events.

The *law of sequentiality*, the time theorists called it. Any alteration of history, no matter how slight, creates an ensuing ripple of change, altering every event after it.

This ripple registered an eventuality warp intensity of point-four on the Dome's scale of historic significance. Not really a big anachronism, by cataclysmic standards, it still was a change in history, and such changes don't just happen. They are caused.

Time travel was like Pandora's box. Once invented, it became a fact, and it would never go away. This was the reason for the Time Enforcement Commission. Somebody had to police time travel, or there would be chaos.

In the TEC squad room, Captain Eugene Matuzek tapped in the codes that awakened the wall screens and individual monitors of the briefing assembly. "Point four," he said. "What do we have on it?"

Dr. Dale Easter keyed in the history section's preliminary findings, and a visual of the Dome's display came up on the screens. "We have epicenter," he said. "Lower Manhattan Island, New York City. Thirteen hundred hours, twelve May, 1930."

"It's in the vicinity of the Brooklyn Tunnel," Amy Fuller added. The pretty historian's dark eyes traced overlays on the monitor. "Between Battery Park and the South Street el, for present coordinates, though most of that wasn't there seventy-eight years ago."

"What was there?" Matuzek asked.

"Streets and buildings. And a lot of social turmoil. The Roaring Twenties had just come crashing down. The Great Depression was in full swing, but the great builders didn't know it. A lot of people had just seen their dreams fly away, but there were architectural marvels rising everywhere. The Empire State Building, for example. It was just being completed."

"Great fortunes colliding with abject poverty." Easter shrugged. "In New York City, the confrontation was sort of violent."

The third historian—and computer expert—in TEC's first-squad ThinkTank, Bob O'Donnelly, grinned boyishly and quipped, "'A meeting of minds and a parting of ways,' as Sinclair Lewis put it." The grin disappeared. "It wasn't funny, in context. The closest event we've found to E-warp's ground zero is a workers' riot, same time and place. That's sort of vague, but there was a lot going on all at once."

"I found a nice visual aid for us," Dale Easter said. A secondary screen displayed an old, halftone photograph of a mob pressing in on a fenced lot while policemen confronted them. It was a city scene. The wide, partially whitewashed brick wall of a building in the immediate background was streaked with soot. An unoccupied scaffold hung there, and beyond the building rose the skyline of 1930s New York.

"From *The New York Times*," Easter said. "I keep files."

"The Treason Papers surfaced about then," Amy noted. "And it relates. Diggers at a construction site uncovered an old copper chest, with Lord North's letters of marque inside it. The theory is, North was trying to buy traitors among the colonists. Benedict Arnold may have been one of those early contacts. That construction site, where they found the documents, is exactly where the time ripple starts."

"We're on the clock on this one." Matuzek frowned. "Give me your best guess. Is our target those old papers? You think somebody is after them? Why?"

Easter shrugged. "Historical significance," he said. "There are a lot of persnickety genealogists out there. Maybe somebody's mom was barred from the DAR because of what great-granduncle Henry did. Who knows? If you were a descendant of Benedict Arnold, would you want the world to know it?"

"Persnickety?" O'Donnelly grinned. "Where'd you find that archaism, Dale?"

"Finicky, then!" Easter shrugged.

"Right on!" O'Donnelly's grin widened. "Finicky's cool."

"Stow it!" Matuzek snapped. "Do the word games on your own time!"

"I concur," Amy Fuller told the captain, ignoring the other historians. "The Revolutionary documents are our best shot."

Matuzek turned to TEC's systems expert. "How about it, Hemmings? Can you patch ChronComp's overall 1930 data into the sublimator?"

"I've already done it," Claire Hemmings said. Blond hair the color of sunlight framed a pretty face as she turned an angry glance toward the final person at the briefing table. "Slice of life, 1930 style. And I kept it real simple, so it shouldn't confuse anybody."

Without returning the challenge, TEC field agent Jack Logan closed his monitor and stood. "I'm ready," he told the captain. "I can launch in five."

Now what? Matuzek wondered, noticing the distinct coldness between his top timecop and the blond systems analyst. The two were like flint and steel. They could work side by side, at HQ or in the field, and perform like the best team he'd ever had—as long as nobody struck sparks. Now there were sparks.

"It's go, then." The captain stood, thumbed his com, and ordered, "Time-launch! Techs to the timesled, Easter on coordinates. Countdown begins now." He headed for the launch bays, calling back over his shoulder, "Get suited and speed-briefed, Jack. Insertion in five."

His mind aswarm with the momentary turmoil of sublimator speed-briefing—a process he sometimes described as "high-speed force-feed of trivia"—Jack Logan shook his head to clear it, then checked his harness and straps. Even for a seasoned veteran, riding the timesled was no picnic.

The sled trembled slightly as tachyon generators in its tail came alive. Ahead lay a long, reinforced track receding into tunnellike distance—the time-launch mechanism, the very heart of TEC. Though not subterranean, the "tunnel" was enclosed, every part of it carefully shielded from the outside world. Only a handful of people in the world knew of this facility—or even knew that time travel was a reality. TEC was doing everything it could to keep it that way.

All along its length, diminishing into the distance, lights and sensor relays flanked the track at short intervals. Tiny in the distance, fully a half mile ahead at the end of track, mighty armatures stood ready to deliver their burst of pure energy, momentarily opening three of the four dimensions of a quadridimensional wormhole in the timestream.

The fourth element of the equation was the sled itself, provided that it reached Q-velocity, or 2,994 feet per second, by the time it hit the wormhole. Logan had taught himself not to think about what happened if that failed. The dim, fused splotches on the catch-wall beyond were reminder enough.

On the boarding dock, Eugene Matuzek leaned into the timesled's cockpit, glanced at the countdown readings on the panel—the same readings displayed on banks above the bays—and said, "Watch yourself on this one, Jack. I hate these uncertain-target missions, and I've got a funny feeling about this one."

"Like there's more here than meets the eye?" Logan nodded. "I've got the same hunch, Gene. Don't worry. I'll be careful."

"Ready?"

"I'm set," Logan said. "Let 'er rip."

New York City
May 12, 1930

No more than a hundred workmen were involved in the excavation on South Birney, but three hundred showed up in the first hour on the day the work was cancelled. Word had spread overnight that the property had changed hands. The new owners—Winston Banking and Trust—were cancelling all labor and crafts contracts on the new building in favor of a Boston general contractor who would bring in his own workmen.

The first arrivals at the gate on this morning were skeptical. They came with their lunches and their gloves, ready to go to work, but the gate was closed and posted. There were police guards on the street. Skepticism turned to anger when the workmen were turned away, and soon there were more . . . and still more on the way.

Like angry bees, they swarmed from the tenements of the Lower East Side, from as far away as Delancey Street and from the teeming warrens around the Battery—men out of work, men down on their luck, men who had seen their dreams go up in smoke in the crash of '29, then had seen the Winston Banking and Trusts rise like phoenix from the ashes of their own ruin. By nine o'clock there were three hundred or more milling in the streets outside the locked gate. By noon there were a thousand, and at twelve-thirty the trouble began.

The site had held three buildings in an earlier, happier time—an old six-story hotel flanked wall-to-wall by lesser structures. Now nothing remained of these but rubble, and amidst the mounds and piles of broken stone and brick, excavation had begun for new footings and foundations. From outside the main gate, men on rooftops could see all the way across the site, to the south perimeter where steel was already rising for the new building's grand tower.

When a dozen men entered the site from over there, some of them carrying picks and shovels, the word spread and the story grew. By noon, those in the streets were convinced that whole new crews of diggers were employed at their jobs, just beyond the rubble heaps. A few hotheads picked up bats and stones and rushed the gate. More police were called in. By twelve-forty a wavering line of copper shields on blue, brass-button tunics strove to defend posted property against a solid mass of angry men. Bricks and pick handles were brandished before nightsticks, and angry shouts filled the air.

Those on rooftops, who could see across the rubble field, saw the dozen men there complete a hurried dig and scramble away, carrying an old, green-copper sea chest. But those below saw only authority, barring their way to the only livelihood they knew. At twelve-forty-three the first stones flew, and a full-scale riot was in progress.

Faced with overwhelming odds, the police line regrouped, fell back, and spread. By squads, they quartered across the field, forming containment units at intervals. As the rioters broke through the gates and howled among the rubble heaps, they broke into little gangs, milling this way and that, and the squads swept down on them, rounding them up.

Johnny-O was just twenty years old—a tall, sturdy young beat cop of mixed Irish descent. Just three months into a career of service to the force, he was proud of his uniform and enthusiastic in his zeal for law and order.

Trotting in from the Battery Street precinct, he saw the men coming out with the old copper chest. A car awaited them at the corner, and a police escort.

"Get that stuff over to City Hall," someone shouted. "It belongs in a museum, not a free-for-all."

Johnny-O's squad trotted past, into the construction zone, and Sergeant Mills tolled them off to assigned points. "Keep the peace, boys!" he ordered. "Hold your ground an' keep your eyes open! An' stay clear of that dead zone where the steelwork is. Man's chance of comin' out of there alive's about one in ten."

As the mobs broke through the first lines, Johnny-O found himself standing alone atop a fresh rubble heap, above a muddy pit. He struck a presence-of-authority pose, feeling a bit lonely. He knew a lot of the people in those mobs. As kids they all ran the same streets, shared the same mischief, swam off the same East River docks. Mostly those weren't criminals over there, just desperate men venting their frustrations in stupid anger.

"Most men lead lives of quiet desperation," he muttered to himself. "Who wrote that? Emerson? No, it was that woodsy fellow, I think." It was an appropriate thought, though. He was seeing the reality of it before him now, and his heart went out to those ragged men invading this field.

But Johnny-O had a job to do. He wasn't one of them, now. He was a cop.

The mobs spread aimlessly, running here and there over the construction site as tight little ranks of uniforms herded them back toward the work gate. But a few broke free, scattering across the rubbled site, scurrying among the mounds and heaps—more of them than a man could keep an eye on.

He didn't know he was in danger until shouts arose twenty feet away, and a thrown brick smashed into his head. He staggered, the world spinning crazily, and felt himself falling.

Four jeering rioters, seeing the young policeman fall, turned and ran.

For a moment Johnny-O lay stunned in the bottom of the fresh-dug pit, his senses reeling. Then he rolled over, cursed a good Irish curse, and braced himself to climb out. His foot slipped on the moist, black soil beneath him, and a foot-thick slab of muck gave way, dropping him to his knees. He glanced down, then froze and stared. In the boot swath where he had slipped, something glistened brightly.

With strong fingers he scraped at the soil, and it peeled away as old, rotted fabric tore aside. Beneath the fabric lay hundreds of gold coins, gleaming brightly in the shadows of the pit.

"Mother of God," Johnny-O breathed.

He heard running footsteps, and on impulse he raked dirt and debris over the gold to hide it. Instinct told him that the mere sight of this gold could turn a senseless riot into a bloodletting. Just above his head, blue helmets appeared in silhouette against the sky.

"Johnny, boy! You, Johnny-O!" a voice demanded. "Saw you fall. Are you hurt?"

"I'm fine, Mac," he assured. "Bump on my noggin,

nothin' more. But there's somethin' buried here. I need a sergeant to look at it."

"Sarge says hold yer post." Mac nodded. "These darlin' boys have about run out of hooraw, so we ought to be done here soon."

The squad above hurried away, and Johnny-O kicked more dirt over the treasure at his feet. He didn't want anybody else finding it before he could turn it over to proper command. He staggered a little, still feeling dizzy, then turned and gaped as a hole opened in thin air just above the rim of the pit and a man fell through, rolling and tumbling down the slope. Johnny-O tried to dodge, but his legs betrayed him, and they both wound up in a tangle at the bottom of the hole.

Instantly, the newcomer disengaged, stood, and backed away a step. "Easy, son," he said. "I'm police, too. Logan, TEC."

Sprawled against the rubble slope, Johnny-O stared at him. The man who called himself Logan was tall, muscular, dark-haired, and strangely dressed. He seemed to be in his mid-thirties. The attire he wore was a dark, close-fitting suit that looked as though it might hide light armor beneath its texture. It might have been a uniform, but it was like no uniform Johnny-O had ever seen. And the weapon at the man's hip was like no gun he had ever imagined.

What kind of game is this one playing? Johnny-O wondered, his eyes narrowing. *Logan, he says. Logan, TEC. What in the name of sweet Mary is TEC?*

Logan looked the scowling policeman over, decided he was uninjured, and glanced down. His boots had scuffed away some of the debris, and gold coin showed through.

He knelt, careful not to turn his back on the wide-eyed policeman. "Now this is interesting," he said. "Nothing in the histories about gold." Crouching, he studied the trove, noting the ancient, rotted fabric of a sailcloth sack that had once contained it. "This has been here a long time," he said conversationally. "I don't suppose you know anything about it?"

"I don't know anything about you," the young policeman growled, gripping his nightstick tightly as he regained his balance, his eyes on the bizarre-looking weapon at Logan's belt. "If you're police, show your shield!"

"We don't use them where I come from." Logan shrugged. "You'll just have to take my word—" Nearby, there were footsteps in gravel, and Logan stood, turned, and raised himself to look out of the hole.

Fifteen feet away, a young woman was picking her way through the rubble, coming toward them. But as she caught sight of Logan she gasped, then turned and ran behind a stone pile. Logan stared after her, his mind racing. Dark hair tucked beneath a wide, ornamented hat. Stylish postflapper clothing and carrying a loose, floppy purse big enough to hold a footlocker. A striking young woman, pretty face dominated by big, dark eyes . . . He felt he should recognize her, that he knew her from somewhere.

In a heartbeat she was gone, dodging behind a rubble heap and out of sight. Logan shook his head, stepped back from the slope, and stars exploded against his cheekbone.

Johnny-O had run out of patience. He had seen a man fall from thin air, and heard no explanation that made sense. The moment the armed, unidentified man was distracted, Johnny-O used his club.

Logan dropped to his knees, blinded by dizzy pain. The

young cop pushed him back and down, expertly, and crouched above him. "Police, eh? Well, jocko, you can tell them about it down at the station. Then if I owe you an apology, you'll get it."

Carefully, Johnny-O braced his stick across Logan's outflung arms and knelt on it. Then he reached for the gun at the stranger's belt.

Trapped by the nightstick, Logan silently cursed his own inattention—turning his back on a stranger with a stick! Any rookie would know better. Now the young bull had him down, and Logan had a dilemma. He could have escaped the stick-hold easily; there were hand-to-hand techniques that this youngster had never imagined. But any one of them was risky. He might injure or even kill the young policeman.

A wry thought cut through his headache: TEC had made a mistake in recruiting an Interpol agent as its chief of martial arts training. Stella Raines was good—maybe the best—but her techniques were ill-suited to keeping the peace. Cops needed to learn to subdue, not to kill.

With a gasp, Johnny-O's prisoner twisted his arms enough to reach the retrieval unit on his wrist, and activated it. Johnny-O's fingers reached for the strange gun and closed around . . . nothing. The ground beneath him seemed to swirl, like a pool of coalescing colors, like a sewer drain venting downward into nothingness. It was only an instant, but it appeared to Johnny-O that the very substance of the earth had opened up and the stranger fell through.

"What the devil? . . ." he whispered.

Again covering the exposed gold, Johnny-O climbed

out of the pit, covered with mud and sand. He saw a blue squad nearby and turned toward them. Sudden movement caught his eye as a pretty, dark-haired woman dodged between stone piles twenty yards away.

"Here, girl!" he shouted. "Where do you think you're—"

Only for a moment did he see her clearly—wide, startled dark eyes blinking with surprise, as though she had been coming to this spot but did not expect to see anyone here. She ducked around a rubble heap and ran. The policeman half shrugged, then realized where she was heading. Scrambling across debris, he gave chase.

She dodged through a gap in a board fence covered with danger signs, and into the busy, noisy lot where steelworkers were raising a tower. "Fool female's gonna get herself killed," Johnny-O hissed as the girl ducked into the high-hazard area beneath the catwalks. Anybody in New York knew not to approach a steel rise, but she seemed unaware of the danger. Ahead of her, workmen on the ground stood well clear of a dead zone where new steel was being shored-in above. Here and there, in that fifty feet of hell, hot rivets and bits of steel framing showered from above to clang on the pavement below.

The girl glanced back, saw Johnny-O pursuing her, and darted through the clusters of workmen, directly into the dead zone. Desperately, the young policeman followed, putting on a burst of speed, ignoring the warning shouts around him.

Then it was raining metal. A beam swung into place high above, where steelmen danced like acrobats on a wire, and tailings fell everywhere. Johnny-O had one final glimpse of the girl as she fell, then he never saw anything again. A plummeting angle brace—four pounds of inert iron from sixty feet overhead—crushed his skull. He was dead before his face hit the pavement.

TEC Headquarters
2008

Bruised and unhappy, sporting a livid welt on his right cheekbone and bruises on his forearms, Jack Logan slid back the hatch of the returned timesled and climbed out to face a half-dozen businesslike TEC guards waiting for him at the boarding bay. They had their weapons drawn and ready.

"Identify yourself," the leader snapped.

Logan looked from one guard to the other. He knew every one of them by name, but it was obvious that they didn't know him. "Logan," he complied. "Jack Logan, field agent lieutenant grade, TEC HQ." He pinned the leader with his gaze. "That enough, Glen, or do you want name and rank on yourself and your buddies, too?"

Sergeant Glen Malloy stared at him. "What are you supposed to be, mister, a paradoxer? Yeah, real likely! Okay, uh . . . Logan, you can tell it to the captain."

Paradox had gained new meanings with the advent of time travel. It was one of the credos of TEC Academy training that those who dealt with historic change—time-cops among them—sometimes returned to a present-day world slightly different from the one they had left. It was, therefore, always possible that the world they came home to might be a world in which they did not exist.

It was hypothetically rare. In fact, in history as it stood now, it had never happened before. But it was, theoretically, possible. And in a world of infinite possibilities, the unlikely was bound to occur sooner or later.

Logan wondered now, as he was escorted into the familiar turf of TEC headquarters, just what little anachronism in 1930 had altered the timestream so that there was no TEC Agent Jack Logan in 2008. And, equally critical, what else had changed? It was time for a reality check.

The ordeal began with blond hair, blue eyes, and a cranky disposition. Claire Hemmings was waiting for him just inside the concourse, with a pair of TECs and a memcorder.

"Who's this?" she asked Malloy, looking Logan up and down like a side of beef.

"Paradoxer, allegedly," the guard sergeant told her. "Says his name's Logan, and he seems to know me—to know all of us. Logan, this is our systems analyst—"

"Hello, Taffy," Logan rasped. "Better set up an anomaly scan. We're going to need it."

"What did you call me?" she demanded.

"Nothing. Just a nickname from another time."

She backed away a step, glaring at him with obvious disapproval. "You know me, do you?"

"Right down to the freckles on your—"

"All right!" she snapped. "Review hearing will decide

whether you're a paradox or an impostor. Where and when have you been?"

"New York City, Lower Manhattan, 1930," he said. "I responded to a point-four ripple. A time alteration centered on the discovery of some old Revolutionary War papers."

"So, if you intervened correctly, how did you manage to wipe yourself out?" Her disinterested gaze summarized him as the TECs checked his vital signs.

"I didn't wipe myself out!"

"Well, obviously something did." She frowned, reached up to touch his temple with gentle-seeming fingers, then thumped the welt on his cheek. "Does that hurt?"

Logan flinched and backed away. "You haven't changed a bit, Hemmings. How about that anomaly scan?"

"What, exactly, is an anomaly scan, Agent Logan?"

Logan's jaw dropped. "Anomaly scan, Hemmings! Your own technique! You developed it after we—well, no, I guess you didn't, did you? We worked together on that, when I was here. But I was never here, now, was I? History has changed, and I'm not in it." He sighed, realizing the enormity of that truth. "My God!"

"So how did I do that—the anomaly scan thing?"

"With the damned speed-brief sublimator," he said. "After I explained to you how that piece of junk was going to kill somebody, you modified it. You and ChronComp. And that led to the anomaly scan. Pretty good idea, really. You backfed the sublimator into ChronComp's mission program after each mission. Historical alterations were part of ChronComp's memory, but not the sublimator's, so they registered."

"Interesting," Claire admitted. "And I modified the sublimator, in your history? I wonder how I changed it."

"For the better," Logan said sadly. "More selective data, less trivia. The modified version didn't cripple us with confusion like the—My God!" He straightened, pivoted, and elbowed surprised guards aside to push through the launch-bay doors.

At the dock, technologists were just boarding the time-sled for inspection. Logan shouted, "You, there! Don't touch that onboard sublimator!"

Glen Malloy's guards were only a step behind him. Now they surrounded him, their weapons drawn and ready. Logan pointed. "Glen, don't let anybody fool with that sublimator. It has vital data in it."

"Sir," Malloy said, "please return to the bay foyer before I have to shoot hell out of you."

"No problem," Logan said, and shrugged. "For the record, Sergeant, this is AXT-CON direct command number 409G: No one is to remove, reset, or in any way alter that sublimator pending further orders."

Back inside TEC, Logan was herded toward the briefing room for interrogation. Claire Hemmings hurried to catch up. "What's that AXT-CON command business?" she asked. "What does that mean?"

"I just made it up." Logan shrugged. "TEC may be top secret, but it's still a bureaucracy. Anything with a number on it has to be processed before it can be rejected. AXT is, as you know, the mother command program for the whole system. If Glen tries to run AXT-anything through Chron-Comp, he might as well sit back and relax, because ChronComp is going to tell him all about itself in great detail."

Claire shook her head. "You're serious about that subli-mator thing, aren't you?" she mused. "You think it might work?"

Logan nodded grimly. "That sublimator was in the timesled while I was in 1930. It's still there, so it wasn't affected by the time-line change. Its program might—just might—be the same as it was when ChronComp pro-grammed it for my mission—before history was altered. If I remember history as it was before—when I was part of it—maybe the sublimator remembers it that way, too."

Flanked by guards, they headed for the briefing room, Logan leading the way.

"What about CON?"

"What?"

"You told the sergeant that made-up command was AXT-CON. What's CON?"

"Actually," Logan admitted, "it was a semantic thing. Some ethnic street slang from a previous mission. Sergeant Malloy's a by-the-book cop. He wouldn't have put a seal on that sublimator just because I AXT him to, so I had to CON him. The 409G part is—was—the mission number."

In a quiet alcove just off the Dome corridor, Logan hes-itated a moment, lowering his head. Here, flanked by flags and drapes, were the inscribed, solemn memorials of TEC's eternal honor roll—names and gravures of those who had gone out in defense of history and not come back. It was a habit with Logan, stopping for a moment before the solemn roster. But as usual, he didn't really look at it. There were names and faces there that he would never for-get—faces better seen in living memory than in zinc-and-bronze replica.

Above the display was a simple title: KILD. Killed in Line of Duty. Logan closed his eyes and shook his head sorrowfully. "Harriet," he muttered. "Damn, Harriet! I miss you."

Beside him, Claire Hemmings asked, "Who?"

In surprise, he looked up, really looking at the memorial for the first time. "A partner. Harriet Blevins. You know. She died in . . ." But there was no such inscription there. "Of course." He sagged. "Of course she isn't here. She's part of my past, and my past never happened."

Maybe somewhere—in this version of history—there still was a Harriet Blevins. And maybe her code name was still Angel. But he had never been part of her life, any more than that of the small, blond woman standing beside him now.

Logan had been running on adrenaline since the New York mission. Now, suddenly, he felt very tired.

The difference between debriefing and interrogation in a postmission interview depends upon who the subject is. As TEC's ace field investigator, Officer Jack Logan would have been debriefed. As an unknown person in obvious possession of a great deal of classified information about the world's most secret organization, he was interrogated.

Fortunately, the possibility of a timecop returning to a world altered by probability—a world in which he did not exist—had been considered and accounted for in the early development of the Time Enforcement Commission.

The closed hearing conducted by Captain Eugene Matuzek—TEC's first and only chief administrator— lasted more than four hours and included the heads of all divisions of the agency. The inquiries were thorough and exhaustive and included subliminal analysis as thorough as that of any academy candidate.

But at the end of it Logan was accepted as who he was. The deciding factor was the mission sublimator. It was program-specific for him, bits and pieces of a past from his viewpoint, and its subliminals could not have been faked.

Logan's authentication was proposed by Matuzek and would be confirmed by Charles Graham, chief of the National Security Agency's Black Ops section.

Jack Logan was now, officially, a paradox. Some alteration had occurred in history, and in present history he did not exist. There was no Jack Logan. He had never been born. Yet, because of being "out of time" at the moment history changed, he was still here. It was the kind of puzzle that kept TEC theorists up at night.

When it was done, the briefing room cleared until only a few remained. They looked at one another around the big, monitor-laden table—TEC's chief, the head of the history division, the systems analyst, the computer expert, and the man none of them remembered from a past that never happened in their present reality—and Captain Matuzek spread his hands.

"All right, Jack Logan," he said. "You're who you claim to be. You're a senior field agent, with TEC tenure from year one, and we'd all know you like a brother if we remembered you. We'll get you requalified under TEC Academy, then I'll hear your oath and we'll put you to work."

"I already took my service oath."

"Not in this life, you didn't. Whatever the ripple was that got you sent back to 1930 is history now, and we have a paradox. We can square you in the records, but you still don't exist in the day-to-day world. You don't have a past, a private life, a circle of friends, a bank account, a home address, or a car. Hell, you don't even have a place to sleep! So what else can we do with you, but put you to work?"

Logan crossed his arms on the table, giving the captain a cynical gaze. "Go ahead and say it, Gene. There aren't any options in this job, are there?"

"No," Matuzek admitted. "TEC security takes priority. Either we put you to work or we put you away. A charge of historic alteration before Timecourt . . . prima facie with your own testimony as evidence . . . I'm sorry, Logan, but that's just how it is."

"I know." Logan nodded. "At least that hasn't changed."

"We might do a model of his original history, Captain," Dale Easter suggested.

Matuzek glanced at the historian. "What's the point of that? You know as well as I do, there's only one history. Whatever probabilities might have been changed, this is history now, and we're not going to change it."

"Think of it as an exercise," Easter said. "Our theorists have always wanted to test the alternate-reality equations, and here's a chance to do that. Logan's past and the past as we know it—it could be textbook research. And maybe we'll learn something to keep us a step ahead of the dabblers."

"There's also standing order number nine," Claire

Hemmings pointed out. "TEC is partially funded as a research project, isn't it? Well, this would be research, for the record."

Matuzek shrugged. "Okay, how would we proceed?"

"We can try to re-create his history," she suggested. "That sublimator idea just might work. There isn't really much memory in a sublimator bank, but there is a sampling there of what ChronComp knew about 1930, in the 2008 that disappeared. Maybe there's enough for a scenario module, and maybe ChronComp could extrapolate a history from that."

"Easy for you to say," Bob O'Donnelly drawled. "You're talking major cybernetics here. First we've got to figure out how to get ChronComp to accept its own incorrect data without correcting it, then we've got to give it a whole new extrapolation language—like open-ended analogy with a universal base. ChronComp's a huge system, but it's still just a computer. We'll be asking it to compare itself as it is to itself as it might have been, and initiate infinite logic progressions based on the assumption that what it knows is wrong just might be right. The only way I know to even begin that is to infiltrate the basic system diagnostics with an alternate mode and set up parallel loops—"

"Okay, okay!" Matuzek squinted like a man besieged. "Can you do it?"

O'Donnelly grinned and shrugged. "Piece o' cake."

"ThinkTank can review the alternate sequences as they're projected," Dr. Dale Easter suggested. "We could generate some reasonable scenarios, I suppose. But what good does that do us? Say we get a good look at some alternate histories, what changes? A paradox is still a paradox."

"We're looking for clues!" Claire Hemmings pressed. "We need to know what, exactly, caused the change in history that erased Agent Logan. And what else was changed? Alternate means different. We compare scenarios and focus on the differences, right back to the point where history was changed. Maybe at least we can find out what changed it, and why."

"That's a tall order, logistically," Easter noted. "The situation Agent Logan described was complex—a labor riot, recovery of some Revolutionary War documents, a major building under construction, not to mention an undocumented buried treasure in antique gold coins. Then we have unexpected intervention by a city policeman, and an unidentified woman in 1930 who 'looked familiar' to a timecop from 2008 . . . It's a real can of worms. E-warp had to register a temporal anomaly, or there wouldn't have been a ripple. But the ripple has passed and now it's history. If there was an illegal time jumper there, and there must have been, we have no idea who it was."

"A lot of excuses for failure," Claire muttered. "The fact remains, the agent had a job to do and he didn't get it done, and we have his mess to clean up."

"My mess?" Logan had been half-asleep, but now he shot a fierce gaze at the systems analyst. "I'm not the one who never revised the sublimator because I didn't have somebody around to tell me to!"

Claire bristled visibly. "Are you suggesting this mess is my fault, Officer Logan? That's absurd! Even in that alternate reality, the sublimator had nothing to do with your failure to—"

"Whoa!" Matuzek growled. "What's the matter with you two? We're here to solve a problem, not practice hostilities."

Claire reddened and lowered her head. "Sorry, sir. That was unprofessional. I seem to find Officer Logan extremely irritating, even though I hardly know him."

Logan shrugged. "My fault, Captain. I do know Officer Hemmings, and she's one of the most aggravating females I've ever met, but that's no excuse for—"

"Aggravating?" Claire flared at him. "Logan, you'd aggravate the ears off a—"

"Cool it!" Matuzek snapped. "Whatever this is about, shelve it! That's an order. Is that clear?"

"Yes, sir."

"Yes, sir."

"Then let's get on with it," Matuzek growled. "I'll document this project as research, provided it doesn't in any way interfere with our real purpose. Dale, you can get started on a spot review, 1930 to the present. Bob, go to work on ChronComp. Claire, the sublimator is your baby. Get on it and stay on it. Take it home if you have to, but get that memory out where O'Donnelly can use it."

Jack Logan had turned away, trying to stifle a yawn, and Matuzek pointed an authoritative finger at him. "Jack, you're off the clock for temp lag. I'll schedule you for a complete workup—history scan, culture scan, current events, all of it, but you're no good fuzzy-headed. Go find a bed and get some sleep."

"It isn't just the sublimator, Captain." Claire Hemmings frowned. "There are two data banks on the original history—the sublimator's memory, and Logan's memory. I'll need access to both."

"Fine." The captain nodded. "Take them both home with you. Logan can sleep at your place."

"Just like old times," Logan muttered with a sleepy grin.

"Now hold on, Logan!" Claire snapped. "If you've got any ideas . . . I don't know what you and I might have been in your past, but you don't exist in mine. Don't get notions!"

"Déjà vu all over again," Logan said, to no one in particular. "Only before, we slept at my place."

Toronto, Ontario
September 19, 1933

No amount of planning, no subterfuge or elaborate misdirection could truly shield the transfer of a treasure of any historic magnitude from one private owner to another.

The gold itself, under the new socialist regime in the United States, would bring only a fraction of its world market value even if it could be sold without being simply confiscated by the government. But outside the U.S., it was a different story. The rest of the world still had a pre-Roosevelt gold market, and a lively market for illicit antiquities.

The planning began the night Harry Sheffield came home from another ten hours of playing for drunks at Dominic's, to find his young wife sitting on the floor of their Brooklyn walk-up, counting and stacking gold coins. She was using one hand, favoring the other where a livid bruise darkened her shoulder. Amazed and aghast, Harry pressed her for information.

It was like questioning a wall. All Kaki would tell him was that the treasure was theirs, for their future, and that it didn't belong to anyone else. "I didn't steal it, Harry," she assured him. "I found it, crossing a building site. Bruised my shoulder there, too, but it's all right. Only a bruise."

"But all this—!" he gestured. "This is—this is gold! Where—?"

"Harry, it's all right!" she assured him. "It isn't stolen or anything. I just found it. If there's a crime here, it's only trespassing. Nothing more."

Studying the coins, Harry had to admit they didn't look stolen. They just looked . . . old. There were various sizes, thicknesses, and inscriptions. Some were as small as a dime, some larger than a dollar, and there were hundreds of them.

For the first time, looking at them beneath the solitary lightbulb in the threadbare apartment, Harry understood the saying, "Nothing else but gold really looks like gold."

Tatters of an old hemp bag remained in the laden trunk Kaki had somehow dragged home, through reeking, shadowy streets and up three flights of stairs. And with only one good arm! Harry guessed the weight of the trove at more than fifty pounds.

It had taken them two months, then, to devise a plan and make the necessary contacts, but they had managed it. Prohibition had fostered plenty of organizations expert in smuggling, and one of these—which now owned several clubs in Manhattan—was centered in Toronto. Everything Harry and Kaki owned had gone into the purchase of a serviceable old Ford, and they had made the drive to Niagara, then up to Toronto, without incident.

Only in Toronto had Harry become nervous. Dealing with shadowy men in strange surroundings made him itchy—like the nights at Dominic's when the hoods were around. And even though they parted with their treasure at a third its probable value, still the price was more money than he had ever seen or even dreamed of. He had the feeling that they were being watched, or possibly followed.

Kaki's solution was a simple one. Heading southward out of Toronto, they stopped off at a glittering showroom in Burlington, then switched back and headed northward, Harry's grin widening each time he discovered a new thing about the purring new Chrysler sedan at his command.

They made an excursion of it, taking side trips and seeing the scenery all the way up Lake Ontario. They reentered the U.S. at Wolfe Island, and Harry would have headed back to New York City. But Kaki smiled at him.

"We left nothing there," she said. She indicated the plush little motoring cushions of the Chrysler, where nearly a million dollars in U.S. currency was hidden. "You don't have to play the dives anymore, Harry. We have our future ahead of us now, and we can spend it where we please."

"Where to, then?" he asked.

"Where were people comfortable through the worst of the coming decades?" Kaki muttered to herself in that way she had that always seemed to Harry as though she were consulting a private oracle. From her purse, she fished out a gold coin bearing the likeness of some old king. "Heads Carolina, tails California." She giggled. "I'll flip a coin."

Harry gazed at her, fondly as always but puzzled as usual. "Half the time, hon, I don't know what you're talking about. Sometimes I think you came from another planet or somewhere. Like now, what does that business mean?"

"It means we're free." Kaki grinned. "We can go anywhere we want to, and not worry. No dives, no goons, no kickbacks, and no vigorish. We can live, and you can work, and maybe we'll be happy. That's what it means."

"Oh." He smiled, patiently. "You're the craziest girl I ever met, doll, but that's all right with me. Flip it."

"If I were from another planet or somewhere, Harry, would you mind?"

"Not on your life!" He snorted. "You got yourself a white elephant when you pulled me out of that Delancey Street culvert, girl. You're stuck with me, for life. The two of us, together."

"For life." Kaki smiled—that inscrutable grin that Harry had never figured out, that always seemed to mean something more than what was said. "Yeah, I guess that'll do. Between us, we might be surprised how much time we have."

She flipped the coin. With a million dollars in cash and not a worry in the world, they headed out to make a life for themselves, somewhere away from the madness of the city that had humbled Harry Sheffield and almost killed the woman he now loved.

After days of aimless travel, backtracking and sightseeing like honeymooners, they knew they were secure from pursuit. No one except them could possibly know where they had gone.

They believed that, right up to the moment a stranger— with something that might have been a tommy gun but wasn't—blew out the Chrysler's tires on a lonely road outside Vincennes. As the big car skidded into a ditch, the dark figure approached it warily, peering in the dusk. Then he walked up beside it, raised his gun, and fired twice more, through the side windows.

TEC Headquarters
2008

Amy Fuller found Dr. Dale Easter deep in the archives of the TEC library that he considered his "office." Surrounded by the compiled wisdom of ages, he was reading a 1956 *MAD Magazine*. At the staff historian's raised brow, he said, "Cultural research, Amy. I think I'm on the track here of what the 1970s was all about."

"Sure," she said, then handed him a sheaf of printouts. "On the Logan alteration, Doctor . . . we may have found a related anomaly."

"In Logan's alternate time line?"

"No, in our own history. ChronComp came up with it in a documentation search. It isn't much, but does it really seem likely to you that penicillin was developed by a Nebraska housewife, to treat a bronchial infection?"

The question wasn't answered. An alarm sounded through the squad room, and they both raced out of the library. Techs were assembling around the Dome, recording vectors and readings, and Eugene Matuzek pushed through the crowd.

"It's a level one, Captain," an E-warp tech pointed out. "Looks like the source is in southern Indiana, late September of 1933. We're locking on it."

"Give us a run-up on this, Dale," Matuzek snapped at the head of the history section. "Timesled preps! Launch in ten. Who's up?"

"Agent Price is ready at the launch bay, sir," an op-tech said. "She's suiting up now."

Knox County, Indiana
September 30, 1933

It was a lazy Indian summer evening, heavy with the perfumes of new-mown hay, sassafras, and distant wood-smoke drifting through the hills.

Beside a lonely country road, almost hidden in shrubbery, a dark figure crouched, waiting as dusk deepened and first stars came out overhead. Somewhere a lonely whippoorwill called.

The only traffic in the past hour had been a pair of dray wagons heading home from the river-bottom hayfields and a Model T heading for Rock Ford. But now in the distance, headlights topped a ridge for a moment, then disappeared behind a nearer rise, coming this way. In the brush beside the road, the dark figure stirred and raised a stubby weapon. In the shadows, with its rotary magazine and blunt shoulder stock, it might have been a Thompson submachine gun. In reality, it was a gun, but unlike anything else on earth in 1933.

As the approaching car crested the nearer rise, the man

in shadows activated a tracking sight and crouched, alone and waiting.

The quiet of evening was shattered abruptly by a crackling of twigs and the patter of deadfall in the dry leaves of the dark woods around him. A twig snapped, fell, and thumped him on the head, and he swung around, his gun at the ready. But the intruder wasn't behind him. She was directly above him, and as he raised his weapon she fell, crashing through stubby brush, to land directly atop him, flattening him. His gun skittered off into the leaves, and he started after it, then froze as a sharp female voice said, "Hold it right there, mister! You're under arrest, by authority of the Time Enforcement Commission."

Quick, expert hands slipped the retrieval unit from his wrist and snapped a come-along onto his forearms, binding his arms behind him. Then a small, booted foot rolled him over, and he looked up into the business end of an Eagle-9 service side arm with its laser sight centered on his chest. Even in the dusk of evening, he had a clear view of the person behind it—thick auburn hair, the face of a cheerleader, and the uniform of a TEC officer.

"I'm Field Agent Julie Price," she said. "And you really shouldn't have done what you did. Theft by time travel is a grade-one felony in Timecourt, and murder is a capital crime no matter when you are."

"I didn't do anything!" the man hissed. "I was just waiting here—"

"Yes, you did." Julie cut him short. "At nineteen forty-one hours on September 30, 1933, you ambushed a car and killed both of its occupants, in commission of temporal theft." She tipped her head, indicating the approaching vehicle. "That car," she said. "You probably shot out its tires, then killed the people in it and removed approximately one million dollars in cash from their seat cushions."

"But it didn't happen!" the man objected. "The car isn't even here yet!"

"Oh, it happened, all right," Julie said.

Headlights blazed as the car—a new Chrysler—topped the rise and swept past. Its windows were open and its radio was on, a tinny rendition of "Brother, Can You Spare a Dime."

"You'd be killing those people right now if I hadn't stopped you." Julie nodded. "You came equipped for murder, not just robbery."

"All right!" the man hissed. "But this is seventy-five years ago! How did you—just who the hell are you, anyway?"

Julie secured the man's gun and strapped it on her back, then flashed a light around, making sure nothing else from the future was there to find. "I already told you that. I'm a TEC agent. A timecop, from your own time, the year 2008. We stop people who want to mess up the past."

"Timecops?" he whined. "Oh, God! You're real, aren't you! I worked fourteen years on that 4-D field! I'm—I was going to be Father Time! The inventor of time travel! All I needed was a little capital . . . Now you're telling me it's already been done? Oh, Holy Mother! How many other people know about time travel?"

"Too many." Julie completed her site inspection and snugged the come-along to her belt. "For the world's best-kept secret, it has really gotten around. We get first-time inventors like you six or eight times a year. Seems like the first thing every time-travel inventor wants to do is go stumbling around in the past, molesting history. But most of them don't set out to commit murder. Just curious, how did you know about those 1930s people and their money?"

The man subsided, resigned to his fate. "Family records," he said. "My great-uncle bought a coin collection from that pair, in Toronto in 1933. He kept very thorough records."

"That accounts for how," Julie said. "What about where and when?"

"Research." The felon shrugged. "They stopped for gas and coffee at Bruceville, on their way into Illinois. This is the road to the Wabash bridge. Listen, do I get some kind of—of leniency for cooperation?"

"That's up to the Timecourt," Julie said. "Might help, though, if you explain exactly how you made your time jump and where your base is. And I'd suggest you offer the court all the information you researched about those people in that car, and about your uncle's coin collection. There's a computer named ChronComp that just loves information like that."

"When—when do I go to court?"

"Approximately seventy-five years from now." Julie grinned. "About three minutes after I deliver you to TEC, which is right now."

Approaching the bridge across the Wabash, Harry Sheffield glanced again into the rearview mirror, puzzled. To him, the little flickers of ruby light glimpsed at the roadside back there had been a curiosity, nothing more. But Kaki seemed to know what caused the flickers, and her mood had changed abruptly. She sat beside him, deep in thought, and he was concerned.

"Do you want to tell me about it?" he asked gently.

"Yes," she murmured. "Yes, I guess you need to know all of it, Harry. It isn't fair not to warn you . . . if we're in any danger."

The road came down the hill, and the dark woods swept away on both sides. Here the lowlands were cleared, fields frosty-looking under a rising moon. Ahead, the big iron bridge and its railroad twin spanned into the distance, across the dark river.

"What danger?" Harry asked. "Do you still think somebody is following us, Kaki?"

"I didn't think so, but those little red lights . . . Harry, you don't know what *laser* means, do you?"

"Laser? No, I don't think so."

Kaki leaned forward to turn off the radio. "You couldn't know. It hasn't been invented yet. Laser is *light amplification by stimulated emission of radiation*. It's a special application of maser technology perfected in the 1960s . . . thirty years from now. Those flickers we saw back there were laser beams, Harry. Where I come from, they're used for a lot of things . . . including gun sights."

The Chrysler wavered slightly, then steadied as Harry kept his gaze ahead. The bridge rose around them, a dark skeleton of symmetrical iron against the darkening sky, and he concentrated his attention on the narrow lane. The car's hum was staccato echoes through the open windows. Then the river was behind them and they were in Illinois.

"I've never asked you where you're from," Harry said.

"You've never asked me anything," Kaki admitted. "I always knew you wondered, but it isn't your way to ask. Well, I don't really expect you to believe me, but here goes. I'm from the future, Harry. I was born in 1987. Forty-four years from now."

She waited for comment, but he said nothing. In the darkness, she could feel his concerned, puzzled gaze. "It's true," she said. "I grew up in a time half a hundred years in the future, and went into law enforcement—a very special, secret kind of police work. I was a police officer, a rookie cop—it was only my second field mission—but a full-fledged timecop, when I came to your time."

"Time . . . cop?"

"As in time travel, yes. In my time, time travel is a reality. And there are rules, which people sometimes break. I came back in time from the year 2008, to stop a time criminal in 1929. That's what the shoot-out in the Phoenix was all about."

"But that—that was the mobs," Harry managed, trying to follow her, trying to cope with the revelations.

"That was how it seemed," Kaki admitted. "But the truth is, there would have been no shooting if a time jumper from the future hadn't interfered. The man you saw in the corridor—the one you called Bozo—was a jumper from 2008, and my partner and I were there to stop him. But it all went bad. Those trigger-happy goons opened fire. My partner was killed, and I couldn't go back."

"Why not?"

"My retrieval unit was activated. It went back without me. So even if I still existed in the future, after the changes that happened, I was presumed dead—killed in line of duty. No TEC officer would send his retrieval unit back to the future if there was any chance he might survive."

"But I did that!" Harry protested. "I'm the one who set that thing off. It was my fault!"

"It was an accident," she reassured him. "Anyway, I was stuck in the past—my past. And by the time I realized it, it was too late to do much about it. Only one TEC team ever made it back to their own time without a retrieval unit, and the way they did it could have made a shambles of a century of world history if it hadn't worked. They were just plain lucky."

"What—how did they do it?"

"They assassinated Heinrich Himmler. They gambled that a change that big would be caught before its ripples forever changed the future."

"Who's Heinrich Himmler?"

"Why, he's—" She giggled. "No, of course, you don't know. This is 1933. Well, try this: Imagine that somebody from now could go back to 1900 and assassinate Kaiser Wilhelm, or even back to 1850 or so—before the Civil War—and kill Robert E. Lee. What would happen?"

"I guess everything would be different now," he admitted. "Hardly anything would be the same."

"That's how history is." Kaki shrugged. "It's like a long chain of events, every link connected to all the links ahead of it. Change one link, and everything's different."

Harry drove for a time in silence, as the Illinois hills grew around them, shadows in the moonlight. Ahead were the lights of a little town.

"It's—it's unbelievable," he said finally. "But I believe it. Is that how you found the gold coins, Kaki? You knew where they were all along?"

She nodded. "I knew. I saw them on my first TEC mission . . . in 1776. And I knew they were never found. We have—TEC has—a computer that tracks things like that. I found the location after you saved me. A building had been built there, then demolished to make room for newer construction. I wouldn't have taken those coins if history showed they had ever been found, Harry. But somehow they never were. Some documents buried with them were found, but the coins never were. In known history, in 1934 and 1935 a new building went up right on top of them, and the building is still there in 2008. So I really didn't change history by recovering them, did I?"

He would have stopped at Sumner, where there was a little tourist court, but Kaki wanted to go on—to get farther away from the laser flashes they had seen back there. There were no lasers in 1933, and that meant that someone from the future had been there, when they passed. It would be beyond irony, she thought, if some time jumper from the future—maybe somebody who knew about the money they were carrying—were to rob a fugitive from that same future. Of all the people in the world to rob . . .

But those had been laser flickers back there. "Go on, Harry," she urged. "If you're tired, I'll drive. Just show me again how to use the clutch."

He checked the gas gauge and went on. "From the future," he mused. "Well, that explains a lot of things, I guess."

"Does it matter to you?"

"It wouldn't matter to me if you were from Mars, Kaki. I love you. That's all that matters."

She cuddled close to him, letting the rhythm of the wheels and the Indian summer night push back her fears. "I'd better let you in on one more secret, I guess," she said. "I'm pregnant, Harry. We're going to have a baby."

Washington, D.C.
2008

Claire Hemmings drove a plain, commission-issue car and lived in a plain, third-floor walk-up on Twenty-ninth Street. In another life, Logan—who preferred his own powerful Gen-Em Trace—had teased her about the car. But now he didn't bother. In this altered history he had no car at all, or anything else that mattered.

They rode in silence, Logan morose and uncommunicative, not even trying to stifle his yawns as the car wended its way through evening traffic. Hemmings tried to imagine what was in the man's mind—what thoughts and feelings might be churning through a person whose whole world had simply ceased to exist, who suddenly found himself in a world in which he had never existed. There might never be a name for the psychological stress suffered by such a person. Almost by definition, a temporally erased person must be a singularity.

In a way, the TEC systems analyst was encouraged by the signs of exhaustion he exhibited. A quick, furtive check with the car's built-in VS-scan confirmed her theory. Faced with an imponderable problem, Logan was subliminally falling back on humanity's most basic defense. His metabolism was slowing, shielding his mind, preparing him for sleep. Faced with traumatic stress syndrome, he was, literally, preparing to sleep it off.

But arriving at Hemmings's residence, which he had never seen in any life, Logan couldn't resist a dig. Setting the sublimator and its program banks on a cluttered table already laden with systems graphs and twin LPC units, he gazed around at the severe, businesslike decor of the place and shook his head sympathetically.

"You probably don't have any social life at all, now that I don't exist," he said.

She turned and glared at him. "What do you mean by that?"

"This place." He waved a casual hand. "This isn't a home, it's a second office. Is that all you do, Hemmings? Work?"

"My private life is my concern," she snapped. "I happen to like my work."

"And I'm sure you and your systems research make a lovely couple," he drawled. "So where do you sleep?"

"I have more than one room!" She pointed. "That's the bedroom, in there. I sleep there." Fuming, she turned her back and busied herself with the day's collection of memos. Even half-asleep, the man was incredibly annoying.

"Primate!" she muttered. "So what kind of quarters did you have . . . in that other history? Some private little pleasure palace complete with hot and cold running bimbos? Well, that's your problem, Logan, not mine. You're just a test case in system anomaly to me. I'm not the slightest bit interested in your evaluation of my lifestyle."

He didn't answer, and she continued her readouts. After a minute or two, though, she said, "I'm sorry, Logan. I know you're under intense stress, and you're probably exhausted. So why don't you curl up in that chair over there and get some sleep. There are blankets in the closet, and you can use the utility washroom in the hall. I'm just going to straighten up these —" She turned. "Logan? Where the devil did you—"

She found him in the bedroom, sprawled across her only bed, sound asleep.

TEC Headquarters

Like a cybernetic mole, Bob O'Donnelly burrowed and tunneled into the heart of one of the world's largest virtual intelligence–data analysis systems, the worldwide computer network affectionately called ChronComp. Based on an in-house, state-of-the-art megaframe system, Chron-Comp was an enormous webwork of interrelated data chains with taproots into every legitimate intelligence network, archive, and chronicling procedure on earth . . . and quite a few nonlegitimate ones.

The central processing unit for all of this lived in a hermetically sealed vault in the center of a room that—back before the Time Enforcement Commission acquired this several-block section of the old warehouse district and converted all of its interiors into a time-travel law enforcement headquarters—might have been a large cafeteria.

All around ChronComp's vault, and around the walls of the CCU section, techs worked at monitors and consoles. One entire wall of the facility was a bank of screens, readouts, and dedicated links to a huge, inaccessible E-warp nest just a fire wall away.

In a secure booth overlooking the entire operation, a separate bank of monitors attended to the computers themselves, and it was here that TEC's ranking computer wizard had ensconced himself.

"Did you know," O'Donnelly remarked cheerfully as Dale Easter entered the booth and looked over his shoulder, "that if all the learned facts acquired by every person on earth since the beginning of recorded history were all combined, tabulated, and translated into cybernese, they would occupy less than one-eighth of ChronComp's present data bank?"

"Fascinating," Easter drawled. "How's the infiltration coming?"

"Gettin' there." O'Donnelly shrugged. "Interesting puzzle. Like making all of ChronComp into two Chron-Comps without dividing it into separate parts. ChronComp is pretty well programmed to protect itself against dichotomy. Which is a good thing, considering that we could wind up with a schizophrenic computer here otherwise. I was right about the diagnostics function, though. ChronComp has no logic shields against its own diagnostics, so I'm using that avenue to create parallel loops—CCA and CCB. Each loop is ChronComp, and they'll be identical until we begin feeding in alternate eventualities. Then they'll just be twins. Theoretically, CCA—which won't have its data bank distorted—should be able to evaluate the diverging viewpoint of CCB and give us progressive alternate scenarios from any divergence we feed in, or retrogressive analysis of scenarios back to where they parted company."

"Ask a computer nut what time it is, and he'll tell you how to build a watch," Easter muttered. "All I wanted to know was, when will it be ready?"

"Six hours, barring total system crash," O'Donnelly said happily. "When will Hemmings be in with the sublimator data?"

"She took Logan home with her." Easter shrugged.

"So what's that supposed to mean?"

"Maybe they'll be back in six hours, if they don't kill each other before then. The way those two strike sparks, you'd think they'd known each other for a long time."

"They have, in Logan's history," O'Donnelly reminded the chief historian.

Julie Price, fresh from her debriefing after a successful mission back to 1933, entered the data-file corridor to present her tapes to a ChronComp tech. Bob O'Donnelly waved at her and gave her a thumbs-up sign. The auburn-haired timecop waved back. Like Jack Logan, Julie was technically an anachronism in 2008. Sent back from 2010 as a courier a year or so ago, she had been trapped in this "past" for the duration. Unlike Logan, though, it was a temporary displacement. Two more years in the "past" and she would be back where she started. She just had to avoid running into herself in the meantime.

Logan's case was another matter, and Easter pursed his lips thoughtfully as he considered it.

"What would you do if you didn't exist?" he asked O'Donnelly.

The computer expert glanced around. "What?"

"I'm thinking about that guy Logan," Easter said. "It must be a real shock to return to your base after a mission and find yourself erased. Your whole life, every association you've ever had, everything you've ever done, just . . . gone! God, it must be awful. And the more you remember about your past, the more there is that just, simply, never happened. I'm not sure I like what we're doing to this guy, using him as a guinea pig in a research project."

O'Donnelly paused to think about it. "I see what you mean." He nodded. "But what can we do for him? Nothing. The past he remembers never was. It's been erased and replaced, and that's just how it is."

"You can't help but feel sorry for him, though. Historical alteration happens, and we deal with it rationally because we're part of the result. But to be outside the time line when it changes, then step back in and find yourself nonexistent . . . Lord, think how that must feel!"

"Maybe at least we can help him know what it was that wiped him out," O'Donnelly said.

"I'm not sure that's a favor." Easter frowned. "Say we pinpoint exactly what happened, exactly what incident erased Jack Logan from history. Then what? You think we're going to change anything? The law is clear on that. We don't change history, if we can avoid it. We don't make tracks. Besides, who'd be willing to undo it, if we could? Original or not, the history we have now is our history."

"Everybody's but his."

"Yeah, everybody's but his. The man has a lifetime behind him that never happened. The world we know is the world without that lifetime, but it's the real world for everybody else in it. Do you think anybody'd take the chance of changing all that? I don't think so."

O'Donnelly thought about it as Easter walked away, ambling across toward the TEC library. He thought about it, then wished he hadn't. With a grimace, he turned back to what he had been doing. Redesigning the logic tree of a megaframe system dealing in four-dimensional quantum theory was intricate work, but it was far less confusing than even the simplest human equations.

"It all looks about the way I remember it," Logan said, frowning at projected images of New York City, spanning the time from 1930 to the present, 2008. "The world's second ugliest city—Whoa! Back up. What's that?" Claire ran the scan back a heartbeat, and Jack pointed. "The building with the gilt dome, just up from the U.N. What's that?"

"Tower of North America," Claire said. "Sometimes known as Porter's Plunge. Why? Is it new to you?"

"Yeah, I think so. Tell me about it."

She turned to her keyboard and accessed ChronComp's NA.Misc files. After a moment's search she keyed a monitor and perused it. "An Am-Can Foundation project, completed in 2001 to house and support the Porter Collections. Port Authority revenue bond funding 80 percent, with joint backing of several U.S. and Canadian trusts. A tax write-off for investors in both countries."

"Porter Collections?"

"Alex Porter, et al," she said. "One of the biggest private collectors of Europeanization memorabilia in the Western Hemisphere. Porter was a British Canadian multimillionaire. Made his money smuggling whiskey into the U.S. in the 1920s, then got involved in armaments during the Second World War. He never surfaced in Canadian or U.K. public affairs, but he was fascinated with U.S. politics. Sort of a friendly, neighborhood kingmaker. He put a lot of money into Roosevelt's campaigns, and made a lot of money underwriting NIRA projects.

"He was an avid collector of British American eighteenth-century artifacts, starting in the '30s with some coin collections that just sort of grew."

The screen displayed lavish, high-security interiors, views of a museum. At a scan of coin displays, Logan stopped the motion. Hundreds of gold coins, various types and sizes, were displayed on velvet under glass. "Those coins I saw on the 1930 mission—there's no record of their ever being found?"

"No record." Claire nodded.

"Memo to ThinkTank," Logan said. "Item: track histories of Alex Porter, the Porter Collections, Am-Can Foundation, and the Tower of North America building, against sublimator data. Item: do an origins trace on the Porter coins."

Claire dutifully keyed in the memos, then scowled at Logan. "Why don't you just concentrate on remembering," she snapped. "Data tracing is my job. I'll do the memos and direct the search."

"Then do it." He shrugged. "You wanted variances between histories, and I've found one. I don't think that building existed in New York before I went back to 1930, and I'll bet my boots against your chiffon undies that there wasn't any Alex Porter involved in the Roosevelt years in my history."

"It does tie in with gold coins," she admitted, then the scowl returned. "I don't wear chiffon undies!"

"I'm sure you don't," Logan said laconically. "You just keep that pink set in your dresser in hopes of an appropriate occasion."

"It's none of your business what I keep in my dresser!"

"Or my concern, either." He grinned. "But I'm a cop. I'm trained to be nosy and observant."

Eugene Matuzek looked up from the mind-numbing stack of paperwork before him as Dale Easter rapped at his door frame. The chief historian took his glance as an invitation and hurried in, carrying an armload of antique-looking tractor-feed forms, which he dumped on top of the stacks on Matuzek's desk.

"There's something here you need to see, Captain," Easter said. "ChronComp's—"

"Dammit, Dale, you know I can't read all that! Where's the summary?"

"Sorry, sir." Easter blinked. "I just thought you'd want to see this."

"Give me the short version, then. What is it?"

"Mission and assignment data for the past year," Easter explained. "In the twelve months ending yesterday, TEC conducted a total of two hundred and sixty time insertions, each involving either one or two field personnel. The total is three hundred forty-four assignments."

"So?"

"Well, sir, Hemmings just linked in her first anomaly check from the sublimator on the Logan mission. The first thing ChronComp blipped was total count, and no wonder! According to the status module in the sublimator, we're running more than twice the number of back-time insertions TEC had in that alternate history of Logan's. Two-point-oh-eight to one! And field staff time allocated is two-point-nine-two to one! It's a remarkable anomaly."

Matuzek stared at the scientist, digesting it. "How do you account for the difference, Dale?"

"It's too early to tell, but two possibilities come immediately to mind. One, there's something in our history, some factor we haven't analyzed yet, that gives us a whole lot more jumper activity than that other history had. Two, maybe our history is, somehow, intrinsically unstable."

"What do you mean, 'unstable'?"

"It's just a thought." Easter shrugged. "Very likely the

difference is in general knowledge of time-travel technology. Maybe in Logan's other history, there were fewer jumpers. It must be something like that! Otherwise, it's like the fabric of our time line has weak places in it."

Without a word, Matuzek picked up a handcom and coded in Claire Hemmings's seek number. After a moment's pause he said, "Hemmings? Gene Matuzek. Ask Logan how many timefields he knows about."

He listened for a few seconds, then frowned. "Okay, thanks. See me when you check in." He put down the handcom and crossed his arms on the stacked papers before him, gazing at Easter. "In Logan's version of history, there are only three legal, legitimate time-launch systems. Ours here, and two tightly controlled research sleds—one in Europe and one in Australia."

"No Am-Can base?" Easter whistled. "God, no wonder things are different!"

IV

Warm Springs, Georgia
September 1927

In heavy shrubs above the manicured lawns leading
down to the health resort's mineral pools, a tall, moon-
blond woman squirmed out of a garment that resembled a
test pilot's jumpsuit reinforced with heavy nylon webbing
and protective pads, and opened a small valise. From this
container she drew a gray skirt, a white cotton blouse, and
a long, white medical coat, which she put on. The severe
starched and ironed garment subdued the muscular, ath-
letic lines of her wide shoulders. There was also a little
packet of hypodermic needles, which she thrust into a coat
pocket.

Down by the pools, a wheelchair rested on the bathers'
dock, near a stage with a strap-lift. A white-coated attendant sat nearby in a painted rattan chair, reading a
newspaper. In the water, a man was swimming—slow,
methodical laps between the dock and a waders' rail fifty
feet away.

The only other people within sight were a dozen or so
up by the resort's clubhouse, where wide umbrellas gave

64

color to a paved, low-walled veranda. Mostly men, though she did see two or three women, including an attractive young redhead just stepping out onto the high lawn. At a corner table near the open north end of the veranda, three men in business suits sat stiffly attentive while a photographer with a tripod-mounted camera focused his lens on them.

The woman in the shrubbery completed her costume change, buried her harness suit beneath creeping vines at the base of an oak tree, and smoothed back her blond hair.

In a paved parking lot adjacent to the club, she surveyed waiting vehicles and selected two—a sleek, powerful roadster and an ambulance.

It was a moment's work to start both engines.

She backed the roadster from its stall, pointed its Winged Victory hood ornament up the drive toward the clubhouse, and eased it around the curve facing the veranda. The car's twelve-in-line engine throbbed sweetly as she idled there, looking carefully at a little folder of old, umber-edged photographs. She flipped a leaf, looked from the photograph to the veranda and back, and smiled faintly. The picture she was seeing was the same one being framed at that moment by the busy photographer.

Even in profile, the observer recognized the famous faces at that table—Louis "Howie" Howe, James Farley, and Harold Ives.

"Campaign publicity," the woman muttered to herself. "Hypocrites! They were always campaigning, even while that demagogue declined to run."

She put the photo file away, put the roadster into second gear, and eased it forward, aligning it carefully. Then she depressed the throttle lever, swung over the side of the open car, and edged away, turning toward the ambulance as the empty car headed for the veranda.

She was in the ambulance, heading down toward the mineral pool, when she heard the commotion above and behind her. The roadster had reached the open veranda and was caroming along its length—scattering people, furniture, and bright umbrellas everywhere. Most of the people there—maybe not all, but most—would escape injury, but it would take several minutes to restore any sort of order, even after the roadster stalled itself against the clubhouse wall.

It was all the diversion she would need.

She drove the hundred yards to the mineral pool and pulled up just short of the bathers' dock. "You're needed up there!" she shouted at the white-coated attendant. "I'll assist here!"

With only a glance toward the swimmer behind him, the attendant ran toward the clubhouse.

The blond woman stepped from the ambulance, strode onto the dock, and crouched at its lip. "A disturbance, sir," she said. "Here, let me help you."

As the swimmer poised at the dock to push himself upright, the woman put a strong arm around his shoulders. With the other hand she ran a needle home and squeezed the plunger. The swimmer flinched, tried to lurch backward, but she held him.

"Who are you?" the bather demanded. "What was that you did to me?"

"An injection," she said. "A substance you've never heard of."

She lifted him easily and pulled him forward, facedown. By the time he was sprawled on the dock, the bathing man was unconscious.

Quickly, expertly, the blond woman half hoisted him and dragged him to the ambulance. As she closed the rear door, she muttered, "Have a nice sleep, Mr. Roosevelt, sir. You'll have nothing better to do for a while."

Before the people at the resort headquarters knew he was gone, Franklin Delano Roosevelt would be beyond recovery. The abandoned ambulance would be found three miles away on the road to Atlanta, but there would be no trace of its occupants.

TEC Headquarters
2008

No living person could truly claim to understand the phenomenon called E-warp. Eventuality-wave theory was a tagalong science that had fascinated many a scholar since its inception in the 1970s, but had gone nowhere. Eventuality resonance in the fourth dimension was a mathematicians' toy—a technology based upon theories that could not be proven empirically for the simple reason that the human mind was not equipped to "see" in four dimensions. No practical application for E-warp existed until the invention of Hans Kleindast's first timesled. Then, abruptly, E-warp had its purpose.

Like the timefield that sprang into existence the instant a timesled moving at a velocity of plus-2,994 fps entered an electromagnetic matrix generated by huge modular-wave capacitors, E-warp's sensitivity to changes in the timestream was beyond sensory understanding. But it worked. "Sensing" history as a progressive constant, the E-warp mechanism could detect anachronisms down to one one-thousandth of a probability and display their source and magnitude as ripples on the great, overhead screen called the Dome of History.

Anachronisms below point-one were referred to as blips and generally corrected themselves without significant historical alteration. At the other end of the scale, a level-ten ripple represented a calamitous alteration of enormous proportion. A level-ten might signal the end of the human race, the destruction of the universe . . . anything! Level-ten was hypothetical. There had never been a level-ten ripple.

But there had been a few midrange ripples since the invention of time travel, and anything above level two was considered catastrophic. Thus when the Dome developed a ripple based in 1927, and the ripple quickly grew to level-four intensity, the Time Enforcement Commission went on full red alert.

Even as the alarm sounded, techs were already at the launch bays, tuning the timefield generators, scurrying around the timesled, and coordinating vectors with the Dome. No assembly was required for ThinkTank. The touch of switches, and all members of the ripple-response team were on direct monitor link with ChronComp and with one another.

Captain Eugene Matuzek arrived at the briefing room only seconds ahead of Dr. Dale Easter, with the vector reports.

"It's a full level-four," Easter confirmed. "We've got zero at fifteen forty-six hours, September 21, 1927, just

outside of Warm Springs, Georgia, and a situation estimate for—"

"Hold on." Matuzek raised his hand as Amy Fuller
and Bob O'Donnelly hurried in, followed by Julie Price
and two other field agents, already suited up for launch.
"Where's Hemmings? And the paradoxer, Logan. Have
they come in?"

"Right here, Captain," Claire Hemmings said, from the
door. "Systems check is ready. We've been on anomaly
scan. It's still running."

Matuzek nodded. "Did everybody get the coordinates
on this ripple? September 21, 1927, Warm Springs, Georgia. Go ahead, Dale."

"We've cross-checked events at that time and place,"
Easter said. "It comes down to one probability—a politician named Franklin Delano Roosevelt. He was named
that day as a candidate for governor of the state of New
York. Anything to do with him could generate a ripple like
this one, because he went on to become president of the
United States. The Second World War was his war."

"He was at Warm Springs in '27 for mineral-bath therapy,"
Amy Fuller added. "He had contracted poliomyelitis—
they used to call it infantile paralysis—six years earlier,
and had only limited use of his legs."

"An assassination, maybe?" O'Donnelly suggested.
"Lord knows there are a lot of people who think this
would be a better world if Roosevelt hadn't happened."

"Possibly." Matuzek shrugged. "We won't know till we
get there. I want a tandem team on this one. Who's ready?
Shanks, you and Taylor? . . ."

"I can take it," Julie Price said. "I'm briefed on the
period."

"My partner's in Timecourt." Agent Shanks shrugged. "I could pair with somebody else, though."

"Logan's ready," Claire Hemmings suggested. At Matuzek's hesitation she added, "He was a top field agent, Captain. And 1927 precedes his anachronism."

"How about the anomaly scan?" Matuzek frowned. "Logan is assigned—"

"Logan's done all he can do on that, Captain," Jack Logan growled. "And he can speak for himself. I'm ready, and I'm already qualified on the sublimator modifications. I'll go."

"Okay," Matuzek decided. "Logan, you're up. But only as secondary. Julie will be senior on this mission. Take it or leave it."

"I'll take it," Logan said, and nodded. "It goes with being a paradox. You don't know me from Adam until you see me work."

Matuzek glanced at Julie Price. "Okay?"

"Fine with me," she said.

"All right, then. You're on, Logan. Easter has the point data. O'Donnelly's on gear-check. Hemmings, you handle the sublimator. Launch in five."

Warm Springs, Georgia
September 21, 1927

A wormhole in time is a time-space vortex, a four-dimensional phenomenon. The fourth of its dimensions is created by matrix insertion at Q-velocity. The TEC timesled slammed down its half mile of track in the time it takes a human heart to beat once, hit the massive energies just short of the farewell wall, and became that dimension.

There are no words in any human language to describe the sensation of the inversion of universal stasis that results in transition from time to time past, and no human synapses quick enough to grasp the reality of it even if it could be described. From massive G-force, the time travelers erupted into another reality, and Logan found himself on his knees, face-to-face with a startled wild boar. For an instant the two stared at each other, both astonished, then Logan flipped backward and shoulder-rolled while the big tusker almost fell over its own feet turning tail. The terrified pig grunted, squealed, and thrashed away through thick brush as Logan came to his feet in a tiny clearing beneath intertwined live oak boughs.

Branches, twigs, and leaves showered down on him from above. "Watch out below!" a high voice warned, and Julie Price swung down from a jutting limb. "Gol-darn space triangulation!" she snapped. "Can't they ever get it right?"

"Just be grateful they've perfected the mass-avoidance equations," Logan suggested. "Otherwise you might materialize underground . . . or inside a tree instead of up one."

They found a break in the forestation and got their bearings. They were on a hillside, overlooking a small, swank resort. A main clubhouse, clusters of bungalows, and a parklike lawn surrounded a series of natural pools fed by hot, steaming mineral springs. Here and there, frock-coated people attended disabled guests, and among the buildings were evidences of medical facilities.

"Warm Springs," Julie said, surveying the scene. "This place could be a vacation spa or a sanitorium."

"Little of both," Logan said, nodding. Then he pointed toward the largest mineral pool, where an attendant was helping a tall, lame man into the water. A wheelchair stood nearby, on the planks of a little dock. "There he is," he said. "FDR himself, at age forty-five. And the fellow with him is his therapist, Frank Osmond. You're senior here, Julie. How do we play it?"

"By the book," she said seriously, accepting command with an ease that brought a grin to Logan's cheeks. Julie was a trained, experienced temporal control officer, junior in rank to what Logan had been in another life but senior to him now, and she took her responsibility seriously. She might look like an auburn-haired Teen Barbie, but there was authority in her glance.

"We inserted a couple of minutes ahead of ripple-point, so we do a two-prong intervention: protect the target, and head off the jumper. A bench warrant arrest if possible, with specifics depending upon evidence of intent."

"That's by the book," Logan agreed.

"I'll take the target subject," Julie decided, pulling a prewrap from her belt pouch. "I'll swing by that clubhouse, then down to the pool. You shadow and back up. Got it?"

She unbuckled her utility belt, opened the prewrap, shook it out, and slipped it over her head. The compacted, web-fine fabric seemed to fill out and solidify as it fell around her, becoming a complete, full-skirted dress of 1920s vintage. With her sunset hair pulled back severely, Julie seemed right at home in 1927.

She rolled her utility belt, thrust it into a shoulder purse, placed her fully loaded BR-9 under the flap—ready at her fingertips—and pivoted once for inspection. Gone was the sleek-uniformed TEC cop. In her place stood a passable Hyde Park debutante—a debutante, Logan noted to himself, with enough firepower to stand off a company of infantry.

"Very good." He winked his approval. "I'll work down to that gate, then back toward the clubhouse. Have a nice time with Mr. Roosevelt, but don't talk politics."

She grinned at the quip, dark eyes twinkling at him. "I probably liked you in that other time, when you were real," she said. "Good hunting."

Following the tree line, Logan skirted the flower beds and manicured lawns, surveying the terrain with policeman's eyes—eyes that saw each detail, missing nothing. He scanned for anything that looked out of place. He was just passing a landscaped hillock topped by a gazebo, on the back lawn of the clubhouse, when he saw what he was looking for—not something unfamiliar, but someone familiar yet out of context. A tall, athletic-looking blond woman in a white smock had emerged from the forest just below him and was walking toward the clubhouse parking lot. Logan glanced at her, then crouched and stared.

"Stella?" he whispered to himself. "Stella Raines? What are you doing here?"

He watched as she inspected vehicles in the parking lot, pausing at an ambulance and then proceeding to a racy roadster near the club walkway. Logan was at the corner of the clubhouse, twenty feet from her, when she started the car and guided it into position, facing the veranda.

She maneuvered the roadster to the top of the walkway, paused for a moment, then set it moving and jumped out.

She was heading for the ambulance when Logan sprinted to the car, heaved at its steering wheel, and headed it toward a stand of trimmed moss rose and cherry laurel shrubs. The car would more than meet its match in that thicket. Not even a tractor could penetrate a laurel stand.

The ambulance was heading for the mineral pool when Logan stepped onto its running board, reached through the window, and depressed the spark lever, killing the engine. The woman at the wheel turned to him and gasped.

"End of the line, Stella," Logan said.

He grasped the door to pull it open, then dodged aside as she struck. Hard knuckles barely missed his windpipe, glanced across his ear, and the ambulance door exploded outward with a force that sent him staggering. Even as he caught his balance, she was on him—a feint, an expert stiff-arm to the chin, and a whirling kick that would have broken bones if it had connected.

Logan backed away, circling. Woman or not, Stella Raines could be lethal. A specialist in martial arts, she had been TEC's chief instructor in hand-to-hand confrontation since she was recruited from Interpol in 2005. Every graduate of TEC Academy, men and women alike, had been taught by Stella Raines. And it was the secret dread of all of them that they might one day have to face some-one like Stella in real combat.

Logan was seeing the reality of that now, as the woman bored in for another attack. She had no recollection of him, of course, but now he saw that even the TEC uniform he wore meant nothing to her. A blur of punishing fists and feet confronted him, staggering him again, and Logan re-alized that Stella wasn't playing games here. She was a time jumper. He had interfered with her, and she meant to kill him.

Still, he hesitated to draw his side arm. Instead he braced himself, blocked a kick to his head and another that could have broken his knee, and waded in, inside the killing range of those fists and feet, to grapple with her and throw her before she could turn his own momentum against him. She broke her fall with her hands and lashed out backward with another double kick. But Logan went under it. As her boots whisked past his ears, he dived, rolled, and swung straight upward, thudding a hard fist into her midriff just at the juncture of her ribs. The blow, delivered from the ground, lifted her and sent her somersaulting.

On driving legs, Logan followed, and as she regained her balance he hit her again, then grasped her head and shoulder and flipped her over his bowed back. He knew a half-dozen recoveries from this tactic, and he knew that she knew more. But just as she hit the ground, he gambled.

"Stella!" he shouted. "That's enough. It's over!"

The gamble worked. Hearing her name from this stranger confused the woman for an instant, and that instant was all Logan needed. Pivoting her face-downward, he caught her wrists in a steel-hard hand and slipped a come-along onto them.

As he stood and backed away, he heard distant shouts, then Julie Price was beside him, staring down at the captive. "Good lord," Julie breathed. "I never saw anything like that! Who is she?"

"You mean you don't know her?" Logan glanced around, puzzled. Julie was a recent TEC Academy trainee—a double trainee. She had trained in 2010 before being sent back to 2007 as a courier, then had retrained in Logan's own time.

"I never saw her before." Julie shrugged. "Who is she?"

"She's Stella Raines," Logan said. "Interpol's best martial arts expert, recruited by TEC three years ago, our time. She's a TEC trainer . . . or she was, in my history."

Kneeling beside the captive, he bound her ankles, then rolled her over. "Check the ambulance." He pointed.

Julie hurried toward the vehicle while Jack flipped his prisoner over again, looking for a temporal control device. As a jumper to the past, she must have brought a retrieval unit to return to her own time. But he didn't see any such device. He found no weapons, either, but then Stella herself was a weapon.

"Stella Raines," he said as he began searching her pockets, "you are under TEC arrest for violation of temporal law. Time travel for the purpose of historical change, attempted murder of a historic personage—"

She glared at him. "I wasn't going to kill him! Just to keep him for a while, until the state election is over."

"Why?"

"To keep the damned demagogue out of national politics! Don't you know what he did? That man condoned monsters! He played global games like they were penny-ante poker, and he allied his country with a monster who murdered millions of people."

"You mean Hitler? He didn't—"

"Not Hitler! Hitler was a pawn, until he broke free from the game and made his own game. I'm talking about the Bloody Beast of Moscow! Without Roosevelt, Josef Stalin would have been nothing!"

Logan shook his head. There were always other ways to

view events. "Do you want to tell me how you got here, Stella? Who helped you penetrate the past?"

She shook her head, her pale eyes blazing up at him. Then with a sudden twist of her head, she grasped the collar of her smock in strong teeth and heaved upward on it, her jaws working.

Logan and Julie both dived for the collar, but it was too late. With a flash of primal powers, the prisoner and everything within several inches of her dissolved into a swirling, coalescing inward spiral of reversing reality, then stabilized, and she was gone.

"Her retrieval unit," Logan muttered. "It was concealed in the insignia on her collar."

"Of course it was!" Julie snapped. "It was an Am-Can unit. They're always miniaturized! They're for covert research!"

There were people hurrying toward them now, from up at the clubhouse, and Logan touched his own wrist unit. "Ready to go home?" he asked.

"I can't believe you missed an Am-Can temporal unit," Julie said, puzzled. "We've all been briefed on them. Didn't you hear about them in your history?"

"I never even heard of Am-Can." Logan shook his head. "But right now, let's move!"

Julie linked her arm in his and held tight. "Let's go," she said, and nodded.

TEC Headquarters
2008

As they climbed out of the returned timesled in TEC's timefield bay, Logan was thoughtful. They had accomplished their mission. The big ripple would be gone, since the anachronism it represented had not occurred. But a new layer had been added to the puzzle of his own altered history. In the history he had come from, Stella Raines had been a TEC training officer. In this history, she wasn't.

This was going to be an interesting debrief.

The ripple was gone. The anachronism had been averted. But Stella Raines was gone, too, without a trace. Background checks identified her as a former Interpol specialist, recruited by the Canadian temporal research project, Am-Can Ltd. But her association with Am-Can had ended a year before, and there was no trace of her present whereabouts.

There was a black-ops report, though, that experimental Canadian timefield equipment had been activated by persons unknown. The obvious conclusion was: Stella Raines. But Stella Raines and who else?

"Add this to the list of differences between my original history and this one," Jack Logan told Eugene Matuzek. "In my history, Stella Raines was a TEC staffer, and a good one. She came on board soon after I did. In this history, TEC never heard of her."

"Correction on that," Matuzek interrupted him. "She never came to TEC, but she was scouted, back when we were just getting started. I know, because I was reviewing all potential recruitees then, with Charles Graham of NSA. I even nominated her for recruitment."

"Then what happened?"

"That was when we were just organizing TEC." The captain shrugged. "Every appointment required three sponsors—Graham, myself, and one field op. Out of every thousand or so recommendations, only one or two were actually recruited. I guess, one way or another, we never got that third signature on Stella Raines."

Logan's eyes narrowed as he remembered. "Yes, you did," he growled. "It was mine. I was on case review for nearly six months of my first year with TEC. Background profiles and judgment calls. I was processing a dozen possibles a day, but I remember Stella's file. I know I forwarded it. So that third signature was mine!"

"In another history, maybe," Matuzek said. "Not in this history, because you weren't here. There wasn't any Jack Logan. You never existed, in this history."

"The chicken and the egg." Logan nodded. The more he saw of a time line that had never included him, the more it haunted him. "Then it was because I wasn't here that Stella Raines went outlaw and almost made a cataclysmic change. For want of a nail, the shoe was lost. For want of a shoe, the horse was lost. For want of a horse—"

"For want of a whole temporal research complex," Dale Easter said. "There's more than just an employment change here. Stella's vehicle to the past was Am-Can's equipment, at Toronto. But, Jack, in your history there is no Am-Can."

Claire Hemmings was at the analysis console, keying in ChronComp's prepared scenarios of prealteration history,

1930 to present, but at Easter's comment she spun around. "I don't see how that's possible! Logan's anomaly—whatever it was—affected his time line, but that has nothing to do with the growth of Am-Can. Where's the connection?"

"Well, apparently there is one. Am-Can is a product of our present history, and it didn't exist in Logan's."

Amy Fuller looked puzzled. "That would imply that the Logan anomaly was a lot wider than we suspected, wouldn't it?"

"Either that, or it wasn't Logan's anomaly at all." Easter turned to Matuzek. "I think we've got something more than a research project here, Captain. Whatever happened in 1930 did more than just wipe out Jack Logan's family tree. Something occurred back then that changed a lot of significant history. And it may still be changing it!"

"This nightmare is beginning to seem like old home week," Logan mused, looking over the displayed data on Stella Raines. "It seems like I know everybody I run across these days, but nobody knows me."

"Is that some kind of paradox syndrome?" Claire Hemmings glanced at him.

"No, it's more than that. It isn't just here, in TEC. I can rationalize the feeling here, because I understand it. But then to jump back in time, and find familiar people there, too . . ."

"Coincidence," Easter decided. "And a lucky one at that. Who else would have been able to ID that perp?"

Logan shook his head. "But that isn't the only one! It seems as if . . . " He tilted his head, his eyes narrowing. "Hemmings, when I put on the subliminator helmet, to have my mind read—"

"We don't read minds!" Claire snapped. "It's just an electronic stimulation of ganglia to bring your memory up to speed."

"Yeah, for speed-reading." He frowned. "But when my ganglia are being zapped, can you capture visuals for playback?"

Eugene Matuzek stared at him for a moment, then tapped a keyboard. "Sorry," he said. "Imagery doesn't translate visual to visual. Why?"

"There was something familiar about that girl I saw on the building site. Maybe if I could see a picture . . ."

"Speaking of the Fister Building location in Lower Manhattan, here's an interesting bit of trivia. ChronComp doesn't have any record of a temporal insertion there in 1930—as you know—but there was one some time back. It went to a different time—1776—but to almost exactly the same location. That data is still being analyzed, but it had to do with somebody threatening the outcome of the American Revolution," Easter interjected.

"Successful mission?"

Matuzek nodded. "Successful. But I don't see any connection to your 1930 mission. Do you?"

"Not off the top of my head. Who had the assignment?"

"A training team—Vince Cole and a rookie named Boyer. Their report is on record."

"I remember Cole." Logan said. "A good cop. Killed on assignment."

"Yeah, on his next mission after that one. He and his partner got caught in the middle of a 1929 gang war. They both bought it—Cole and the same rookie. Their perp died there, too, along with a collection of speakeasy nasties who probably richly deserved it."

"Any connection there to their earlier insertion? Or to my jump?"

"Apparently not. Different circumstances and different cases, entirely. Just a coincidence."

"I believe we have just oversaturated on coincidence," Easter said. "Julie, what were the names of those indigenous people your 1933 collar tried to rob?"

"Sheffield," Julie Price said. "That's about all we have on them. Just their name."

"And the perp you collared, what brought him there?"

"Money," she said. "The robber had decided, from some old family documents, that some people with a lot of money would be driving along that road. So he managed a shoestring jump, lived through it, and laid an ambush for whoever came down that road."

"Anything to the money angle?"

"Who knows? I doubt it. That jumper was a whacked-out psycho."

"Yeah, but there's the gold coin business . . ." Easter scowled through his glasses, then removed them and held them up, looking for lint. "And Toronto."

"What?"

"Your 1933 perp. He testified—well, you were there, Julie. Didn't he say he knew about that money from family records, from a great-uncle or something . . . in Toronto?"

"So?"

"So there was a lot of money coming in from Toronto in 1933. A lot of people from this country went there to sell their gold after the U.S. gold crackdown. And your perp said his great-uncle was a collector in Toronto. One Alex Porter."

"Porter?" Matuzek asked. "As in Am-Can Porter?"

"I saw gold coins," Logan said. "The gold coins that young cop was guarding, on that building site in 1930!"

Beatrice, Nebraska
February 1940

In the central plains beyond Big Muddy, the worst month of the year is February. The shortest month, it is said, is the longest of all. A dreary time in the best of times, and in the worst a month in which sickness can take hold. The Nebraska winter of 1940 bottomed out in a February almost devoid of sunlight, and rampant infection set in.

Staphylococcus, the doctors called it—a bacterium. A germ borne to the homestead hills by migrating workers from Chicago as Beatrice's packing plants expanded. Some of the newcomers had taken ill . . . then more, and the infection had spread. The little hospital was full, and there was talk of closing the schools. For some, those with topical infections, antiseptics and sulfa treatments were effective. But the staph was nonspecific, and for those who caught it internally, there were few courses of medical treatment.

As the agonizing days went by, bronchial infections mounted, followed by stomach ailments and, predictably, increasing cases of pneumonia.

The piano in the snug, modest house on Republic

Avenue—that fine, ebony concert grand whose rich tones had become a fixture in this small neighborhood—was still now. It had been still for weeks, and its silence was one more thread in the fabric of dread that gripped a disease-ridden community.

Few people knew the Sheffields more than casually. He was a local product, raised by a widowed aunt now long deceased. Young Harry had been gone for years, for a time a known pianist in the east, then swallowed by obscurity. But he had returned now, after years of absence—returned with a pretty wife and a child, and with the music that some remembered from his boyhood.

The Sheffields lived comfortably but modestly, though there was rumor of acquired wealth, and Harry spent each day with his music. But now Harry Sheffield was ill— bedfast and suffering from that same raging infection that had stricken so many here in recent weeks.

Dr. Arnesson stopped by on his rounds and did what he could, but he had dozens of other patients now, and there was little he could do. For an infection in the lungs, there was no sure cure. Steam, he suggested. Steam to clear the passages, and a warm bed.

The Sheffields' next-door neighbor, Charlene Harris, had her own thoughts on the matter. Mrs. Harris considered herself a "healer," like her mother before her, and had an abiding distrust of organized medicine.

"Steam's fine," Charlene told Kaki. "Everybody from the Greeks to the Cheyenne Indians has used water vapors. The trick is to mix it with essences like tree moss, sassafras, menthol, and cubebs. Eucalyptus, too, if you can find it. Mustard poultices, kettle steam, and healing essences. And if you can get some fruit, like oranges, they'll help the system fight infections. There's more to medicine than just being a doctor, you know."

Kaki Sheffield listened, and was reminded of something . . . a bit of knowledge retained from scrutinizing the endless, mind-numbing data files of TEC Academy. Oranges. A miracle drug could grow on oranges. At Lindstrom's she found a few rotting, mold-covered oranges. With careful direction she had the pharmacist concoct a fermentation base from the green penicillium mold on the fruit, then reduce the culture to a thick extract.

"It makes an antiseptic," she told the puzzled pharmacist. "An antibiotic that destroys bacteria without poisoning human tissue."

The pharmacist described the procedure to Dr. Arnesson, whose knowledge of folk remedies was extensive but had never included that one. Curiosity took him back to the Sheffield home, and amazement fueled his documentation of Harry Sheffield's swift recovery. He exchanged notes with other physicians while Mrs. Harris, far less cautious, launched a search for spoiled oranges and spread the treatment across several counties.

By the second week of March, the epidemic was past. Harry Sheffield was in touch with his "tune buyers," and the concert grand on Republic Avenue was once again treating neighbors and passersby to melodies that would be heard on the radio months and years later.

"Sometimes I think I should use aliases on these tunes," he told Kaki as he penned in the final notes of a composition for Score One music publishers. "But it wouldn't matter. Nobody notices who wrote a song, only who plays it."

"Does it ever bother you, Harry?" she asked. "Being the 'unknown composer,' I mean?"

"Not a bit." He grinned, putting his arm around her shoulder. "It pays the bills." The grin disappeared. "I only worry that someone in that future time of yours might track us through these songs, might come and take you away from me."

"Not likely, anymore," she said. "It's been almost a dozen years, and I haven't broken any time laws that I know of. I'm not running around causing anachronisms. By now I'm just part of the timestream. What are you worrying about?"

"The penicillin thing," he said. "That could change history sometime in the future."

"That was an emergency." She shrugged. "You were so sick, love . . . I didn't know what else to do. But someone will legitimately invent penicillin before long, anyway, so I don't think the E-warp will pick it up."

"E-warp," he mused. "I've tried to imagine your future science, Kaki: transistors, lasers, tachyon energy, calculators—computers, I mean—that can know everything there is to know and only use two numbers. God, it's hard to envision! Your timefield matrices and the timesled, I can envision that. Even wormholes in time, where dimensions trade places. I've read the theories. But that sensing thing, that E-warp, and the Dome . . . it's beyond me."

"Think of it in musical terms," she suggested. "Everything that happens has its special medleys—notes and chords, like sound but in another dimension, all blending together in a sort of grand symphony that goes on and on. History sings, and its resonances leave echoes. E-warp is attuned to the echoes."

"And the use of penicillin before its time is a false note," Harry mused. "That's why I've been worrying."

Harry Sheffield would never be a famous composer. Fame was a thing he had discarded—and gladly so—the day he fell in love with a girl from the future. But still he composed, and his genius gave the Sheffields a comfortable income.

The treasure that Kaki had found, that had provided the impetus for their life together, had proved unnecessary in the long run. They might have been wealthy by most standards, from the sale of the old coins. But they had used very little of the money. A little seed money, to get started, and they hadn't touched it again. Instead, they had placed it in discreet investments through various Omaha and Kansas City banks—quiet, blue-chip investments to provide a scholarship fund, a future for young James Henry.

The Sheffields lived modestly, in a style that drew no particular attention. Even the place they had chosen to live, the little town of Beatrice, was selected for its obscurity. As a musician, Harry might have been propelled toward the entertainment capitals—places where celebrity waited like a dark, lurking shadow. But as a simple composer of popular songs, he could live anywhere and—with a little care—never be noticed.

Obscurity was a way of life for them. It was the price of peace, for a person from the future. Kaki was always keenly aware—and Harry as aware as a 1940 denizen could be—of the awesome ability of E-warp to spot and target any anachronism in the past, and of ChronComp's ability to track history in its minutest detail. Kaki's very presence in the past, they knew, was a lightning rod that could bring the future down upon them.

But the years passed, and nothing happened. Certainly she was considered dead, back there in the future from which she came. And as certainly, she had avoided obvious anachronisms. Kaki and Harry had become very good at making no tracks.

Still, Harry was right about the penicillin treatments. It was a small thing, but it could start a ripple that E-warp might spot. So when they learned that Dr. Arnesson had corresponded with medical researchers elsewhere, and had arranged tests of the marvelous antibiotic treatment Kaki had "discovered," she went to see Charlene Harris. It was no real problem to convince the healer that mold cultures had been her idea all along, right along with sassafras root, clover honey, and tree moss.

Thus it was Charlene Harris of Beatrice, Nebraska, who was invited to England in the summer of 1940 to assist Sir Howard Florey in the "discovery" of penicillin. There was a bon voyage parade on Beatrice's main street to see the healer off, and the Sheffields breathed sighs of relief.

"How do you handle it, Kaki?" Harry asked his wife. "I mean, in your time there'll be cures for polio and cholera and tuberculosis and—and all those things. How do you live with these things, knowing you could—?"

"I couldn't." She shrugged. "I don't have any more idea how to make polio vaccine than you do about assembling a vacuum tube. I just happened to know the source of penicillin, and Charlene's 'essences' reminded me of it. Maybe history is resilient, Harry. Maybe it has a way of correcting itself, like the S and R people suspect. Maybe Sir Howard Florey did perfect penicillin, in the near future, and Charlene helped."

"Then your E-warp wouldn't pick up any anachronisms?" They strolled beneath spreading elms, James Henry scurrying ahead of them, and Harry mused, "Echoes in history, huh? I sort of understand that analogy. I've heard it said that every 'Ave Maria' ever sung in St. Gregory's can still be heard there, centuries later, if you know how to listen."

In that same summer, James Henry Sheffield, at the age of six, discovered the magic of harmonic resonances while listening to his father's experimental piano chords.

Time Enforcement Commission
Science and Research Division
2008

More than forty people assembled in the high-security conference chamber beneath TEC Central. Half of them were the specialists whose job it was to attend to Chron-Comp, the massive computer system that was the nerve center of TEC. The rest were the historians of ThinkTank, the scientists of TEC S and R, several field enforcement officers, and the head of NSA's Black Ops division.

It was ThinkTank's show, and ChronComp's, with Bob O'Donnelly as emcee. O'Donnelly had completed his "alternate time line" experiment with the huge megaframe, using scenarios generated by the historical section— ThinkTank—and had findings to report.

Even within the TEC complex, which was protected by one of the world's most sophisticated security systems, the S and R section was noted for its impenetrability. Like the double lock on a strongbox, kept in a keyed-bolt locker within the closed vault of an invisible bank, TEC S and R was security within security . . . or, as Bob O'Donnelly called it, a "redundancy of don'ts."

Only once in its history had TEC itself ever been penetrated, and then it was by a TEC agent. The leak had been plugged, and no others ever found. Even that leak, though, would never have breached S and R. Here rested all the technology that made time travel possible, as well as the technology behind every facet of TEC's facility, and it was the sincere intent of all who even knew of its existence that it never be found.

"There is no such thing as a probability line," O'Donnelly told his audience now. "Each probability that occurs, that in fact becomes an event, creates an infinite number of new probabilities. So what we're working with here is a string of judgment calls along a web of potentiality. Producing a picture like this, with cybernetics alone, would have required a computer linkup involving the total processor power of about 50 percent more computers than there are.

"In other words, it would have been a toss-up whether we could even do this, but for three fortunate factors. The first was a surprise. When we started to program a track for an alternate reality, we discovered that ChronComp already knew how to do that."

Several of the scientists from S and R turned abruptly to stare at the speaker. "Knew how?" one asked. "You mean there was already a program?"

"Exactly." O'Donnelly smiled. "It seems our Canadian cousins at Am-Can have been pursuing a similar research. They apparently linked several megaframes on a dedicated-task basis, to work out an alternative eventuality program. ChronComp somehow picked it up and stored it as memory. So when we wanted a random probability scan, it gave us one."

"You said there were three assists," a tech noted. "What were the others?"

"We had a built-in baseline for tracking: the gross eventuality mapping provided by a human witness and an unaltered sublimator chip."

There was some muttering around the table. "What the hell is Am-Can developing alternate histories for?" someone mused.

At the head of the conference table, Charles Graham sighed and raised a casual hand. "Let's roll the credits later, Dr. O'Donnelly," he said. "We all understand the process of eventuality comparison. Cut to the chase."

"You got it." O'Donnelly nodded, touching controls on a console. Around the room, screens came to life. "Two versions of progressive reality, spanning seventy-eight years. The reality we know now, and the reality that might have been had there been no alteration on May 12, 1930— the reality that Agent Jack Logan remembers, because it was his reality.

"We set up a parallel continuum in ChronComp's programming, inserted every scenario and conjecture the history gang could come up with, validated by data from Agent Logan and from a mission sublimator that was programmed in prealteration 2008 for Logan's mission to 1930. Then we had ChronComp's second self construct a history based on these data, and compare that history to our own history. Finally, we ran backscans along both scenarios to see what changed what. We have mixed results."

Dr. Dale Easter glanced up from the monitor where he was skipping ahead of O'Donnelly's narration. "That's putting it mildly," he noted.

Graham raised one eyebrow in that characteristic way

that could make presidents and ambassadors flinch. "Mixed? Mixed how?"

O'Donnelly keyed in symbols. "We have a pretty good idea of why history changed that day in 1930, and some ominous indications of continuing drift—as though there is an ongoing anachronism. It has to do with a treasure in buried gold coins: a war chest of gold, to pay British spies and saboteurs among the American colonists in 1776. Historically, the coins were never found. We have reason to think, now, that they were uncovered—by someone from another time—and that the resulting changes in the timestream are still going on. A rampant paradox, if you will, that surfaced May 12, 1930, on Lower Manhattan Island.

"The mixed part is, we have no evidence of a time-jump insertion on May 12, 1930, except Logan's own mission. And we have no idea why Jack Logan's existence was wiped out in the process."

"That mission," Graham asked, "what was its purpose?"

Across the room, Jack Logan raised his head. "A point-four ripple, sir. Centered at thirteen hundred hours, twelve May, 1930, Lower Manhattan where the Fister Building is now."

"A variety of occurrences coincided there and then." Dale Easter took up the narration. "The Treason Papers were discovered that day—letters and documents from King George's war minister, Lord North. An old copper chest, buried beneath rubble. Letters of marque for collaborators among the colonists. Also, it was a construction site, and there was a labor riot that day. Noisy, and a few casualties, but nothing planned. Just a spontaneous riot. There were a lot of those back then.

"But within a hundred yards of the site, there was another occurrence that seemed unrelated. Two people—a young woman and a rookie cop—tried to cross a dead zone where high iron was going up. Both of them were hit by falling debris. The woman survived, but the policeman was killed. ChronComp makes it 89 percent likely that those were the same two people Officer Logan encountered upon insertion into 1930. Unfortunately, we don't have photos of either of them for a positive ID."

"We have this." O'Donnelly keyed up a picture—an old, posed group photograph. Twenty young men stood shoulder to shoulder in three rows, all wearing 1930-style police uniforms so stiff and new that the screens almost smelled of starch. In the old halftone, their facial features were barely distinguishable. "Third from the left, back. Logan thinks this might be our rookie, though he can't be positive. It's probably him, though. The records match."

"His name was Jonathan O'Hara." Easter said. "He was a 1929 recruit, Battery precinct. A beat patrolman, fresh out of training. On M-day, May 12, 1930, he was twenty years old and assigned to riot detail at the Fister site. They called him Johnny-O. Six feet tall, dark hair and blue eyes, unmarried, good training reports with one exception. He seems to have been a 'sudden' sort, a little impulsive and headstrong. Tended to make his own judgments and act on them, and devil take the hindmost."

"Yeah, tell me about it," Jack Logan muttered.

"What became of him?" Graham asked.

"He died that day. He was the policeman who tried to cross the dead zone. Falling debris crushed his skull."

"And he doesn't track to the anachronism?"

"Not that we can pinpoint, except that his interference

cost Officer Logan the mission. Whatever happened there that day, involving a jumper, went uncorrected."

"Who was the other casualty? A young woman, you said?"

"No ID at all." O'Donnelly shrugged. "Police records have a description—young, dark hair and eyes, attractive. That's all. Workers at the site tried to help her, but she apparently wasn't badly injured. She walked away, and nobody saw where she went. It's very likely she never even knew that a police officer had died in pursuit of her."

"The treasure, then," Graham pressed. "Those gold coins . . ."

"We believe the coins are the key," Easter said. "We know about them only from Logan's observation, but some old British records ChronComp came up with verify that a sailing vessel named *Heron* burned in New York Harbor in 1776, and its manifest included the copper chest that contained the Treason Papers, as well as an unspecified shipment of coins consigned by Lord North. The papers were found on May 12, 1930. They're in the National Museum of History. Our conjecture is that the coins and the papers were buried together, but after the chest was found, a time jumper found the coins—within a few hours of the time Logan saw them there—and took them."

"But why would he leave the loot in its own time?" Graham wondered. "Why not bring it forward with him? Its value would be much greater now."

"That's where it gets really odd," O'Donnelly said. "There's some evidence that those coins found their way to Toronto, into the possession of Alex Porter."

"Porter," Graham breathed. "Porter's Plunge. It was that old pirate's fortune that originally funded Am-Can."

"Circles within circles," Easter said. "Am-Can apparently was the source of our latest temporal emergency—a level-four. A jumper named Stella Raines attempted to kidnap Franklin Delano Roosevelt before his political career got off the ground. Logan and Julie Price successfully aborted the attempt, but the perp managed to jump back to the present. She's still at large."

"Logan recognized and identified Stella Raines," Eugene Matuzek put in. "In his history, she was TEC's ace instructor in hand-to-hand conflict. In our history, she was scouted by TEC but never recruited. That's directly traceable to Logan's absence."

"On the business of the coins," Julie Price noted, "I arrested a jumper on a 1933 ripple. He was a solo flyer, a one-shot. But the people he tried to rob in 1933 were a young couple traveling cross-country. The perp believed they had a large amount of cash in their possession, from the sale of those same coins to Alex Porter in Toronto."

"The couple?" Graham asked.

"Mr. and Mrs. Harry Sheffield, from New York." Julie Price screened a computer trace chart. "He was a piano player, played in various clubs during Prohibition, then just dropped out of sight. ChronComp found a hundred and sixty-one contemporary Mr. and Mrs. Harry Sheffields through census records, but none of them ever came to official notice. No celebrity, no ostentation, no criminals or politicians—just people. Apparently our couple lived out their lives in seclusion somewhere, whoever they were."

Quietly, across the room, Jack Logan stood, turned, and slipped out. Watching him go, Claire Hemmings understood. The room was now full of lighted screens, many of them scrolling views of ChronComp's alternate scenario, which was Logan's own world of now. She tried to imagine the hopelessness of watching these images of one's own whole world, and knowing that it was gone.

Charles Graham glanced at the closing door, and also understood. There was nothing more for Logan to do here, and he had already been through it all. His memories were part of it. "Did you consider a full data sweep on all of those Sheffields?" he asked TEC's captain.

"No, sir, we didn't," Matuzek said. "Except for idle curiosity, we had no reason to. Julie's intervention was by the book. She didn't leave tracks. It's doubtful that those people ever knew they were about to be attacked by a time traveler. And as for his idea that they were carrying money, there was no indication of it except the perp's testimony. Timecourt records show him as a crackpot, and probably delusional."

"All right, so what do we have?" Graham drawled. "An exercise in paradox, but what else? We don't know why Officer Logan fails to exist in our history, and we don't know what happened to the British treasure. What do we have, beyond some questions about Am-Can's timefield research?"

"We have a temporal instability, sir." Captain Matuzek frowned. "We have a time track that seems to keep changing in minor ways, almost day to day. We have two to three times the number of ripples that our alternate scenario seems to experience. And we need to know why."

"There's a bug in our history," Bob O'Donnelly quipped. "Like a system virus."

Dale Easter removed his glasses and squinted at them, then produced a cloth and began polishing the lenses. "It's as though we have an anachronism somewhere in our present fabric, that keeps going on and on without correcting itself. History is fairly resilient, Mr. Graham. Little alterations generally balance themselves out, without major alteration. That's why we rate the ripples that show up on the Dome. Certainly every historic change affects someone, but not many of them are likely to affect everyone. The only way a ripple can just go on and on is if the cause of it is still a factor in historic alteration."

"Such as? . . ."

"Such as—" Easter shrugged. "—say, a repeated manipulation of events by successive time jumpers. Or a time jumper who didn't come back, but remained in the target time. A person out of time is an anachronism, just by his presence."

"Could that happen?"

"I don't see how. If nothing else, the initial insertion would be in ChronComp's data banks."

"Not if those data banks change each time history changes. How do you know, for instance, that our history is changing now?"

"I can answer that," Matuzek said. "Our systems analyst, Officer Hemmings, recovered the data wafer from the sublimator aboard Logan's 1930 launch. Its data and Logan's own memories, enhanced by subliminal stimulation, gave us the basis for our time-track comparison. Then Hemmings carried the experiment a step further. Since Logan's return, ChronComp has compared every returning sublimator wafer against its present data universe. Also, we have done two blank insertions—unmanned, momentary penetrations of time—just to test these comparisons. In every case, there have been minor discrepancies between the history that ChronComp downloaded to the sublimator and the same history on file when the sublimator returned. That's how we know."

"We're getting ready to do it again," Claire Hemmings advised. "If we have a ripple within the next eight hours, there'll be a second onboard sublimator, full of as much reference data as we can pack onto a CW at launch. Both this and the speed-brief wafer will be cross-compared against ChronComp's banks upon return. If there's no ripple, we've scheduled a blank launch for the same purpose."

"I see." Charles Graham crossed his arms on the table before him and lowered his gaze. "*Tempus* rampant," he mused. "A virus in time." He raised his head. "I'd like to see the divergences," he said. "Show me what Chron-Comp saw when it looked at its alter ego."

Dejectedly, Jack Logan strolled through the big squad room of the Time Enforcement Commission. For the first time in his life, he felt lost and helpless. Everything around him here was familiar, but nothing was the same. Over and over, he kept thinking of the family tree Chron-Comp had sketched for him—a tree that didn't have him in it.

His parents weren't there, at least not as he remembered them. There were Logans, but not his line. Three of his grandparents were there, but not the fourth. There was no record of Grandpa Sean. Yet all of his great-grandparents were on the printout. The ones who left him his name—Logan—had even lived in New York. Carl Logan had married Maude Sutton there, in 1932, in a little church only ten blocks from where Jack had landed two years earlier on the time jump that changed his life.

Carl and Maude had produced four sons, but none of them were Jack's grandfather Sean. The line that led to Jack had ended there. He didn't exist. In this history, he had never been born.

He found himself standing before the solemn KILD memorial, gazing at the names and faces of TEC officers killed in line of duty. These had been real people once, even in this new history. They had died, but before that they had lived.

His gaze lingered on a face there, slid away, then snapped back. Suddenly alert, he stepped closer to the stone and read the inscription, memorizing it. Officer Mary Katherine Boyer, 1987–2007, PD.

PD—presumed dead!

Logan was almost running by the time he got back to the S and R conference room and burst in. The door slammed behind him as faces turned to gawk at the intrusion.

"Mary Katherine Boyer!" he announced. "The girl I saw at that building site in 1930 . . . that was Kaki Boyer!"

Paxton Peak, Colorado
August 1971

In a quartz cavern behind a waterfall, hair-fine sensors clung like little black bells to a hundred surfaces, sending silent messages back to the central receptors mounted on a foam-vinyl pad in the vaulted main chamber. Battery-fed work lights around the display console bounced rainbows off the crystal walls, lighting the faces of six young men gathered around the monitors there as scrolling sequences on one screen kept time with the dancing graphics on another.

"Do you see the analogy?" Mac Wainwright indicated a slowly rotating dimensional graph—like an animated picture of a stubby cylinder with sharp peaks and valleys developing on its upper end. "It's a three-axis resonance pattern, very much like a synthesizer chart, but there's no sound involved. We're not measuring any known frequency of harmonics here. We've run disrupts all the way from microwave to ELF—the whole resonant spectrum—and they don't impinge in any measurable way."

Dr. Jimmy Sheffield scowled, concentrating on the

display as though reading its message. "Multiple and variable wavelengths?" he suggested. "I can't see this as anything other than wave phenomenon, Mac. It isn't a picture of rock texture or stress patterns. It's more like a digital interpretation of orchestral music . . . like a picture of how a symphony sounds."

"That's what we thought, too." Charlie Wang nodded. "It's why we first contacted you. But we're puzzled by that regular, recurring gap in the continuity of the waves. Whatever we're looking at here, we're only seeing part of it."

"I see that," Jimmy agreed. "If this were music, it would be cutting in and out . . . like a loose connection in the sound circuits. It's only in the wave pattern, though. The base resonances are constant."

He leaned closer to the screen and adjusted a control. The rotating dimensional graph responded, its vertical lines sprouting a pattern of horizontals that amplified the curving, undulating pattern of its "wall."

"Optical illusion," Wang breathed. "Those textures continue . . . but where do they go?"

"They double back," Jimmy observed. "Back upon themselves, but in—well, some other direction. Some direction off the screen."

"It's a two-dimensional screen." Mac grimaced. "We can image three directional axes. How many directions are there?"

"I'm brainstorming," Jimmy said. "It's as though this equipment is trying to show us something that it doesn't have the vocabulary to reproduce. Have you tried this with a true 3-D matrix?"

"We took the first readings over to Boulder," Mac said.

"Their big computer is a CY 220. They can generate a hologram. The results are spectacular visual effects, but it comes to the same dilemma. Continuous sequences that just . . . disappear without losing continuity. The patterns go off in directions that don't even exist, logically. I mean, after up and down, forward and back, right and left, what? What else is there?"

"Just what the hell have you guys gotten into here?" Jimmy asked, staring at the hypnotic, strangely beautiful convolutions turning grandly on the monitor screen. The illusion of doubling back was breathtaking. It was like looking at a mesmerizing harmonic rhythm and seeing only part of it, but knowing that the rest was there.

Mac sighed. "We're hoping you can tell us that," he said. "You're the expert in harmonic behaviors."

Jimmy tore his gaze away from the screen. "I'll do my best. Your telegram indicated that you just . . . stumbled across this anomaly. What were you looking for, anyway?"

"Echoes and imprints." Wang shrugged. "Sensors that sense and record, but who knows what they're sensing. Are you familiar with Infeld's theories of perpetual resonance? Fascinating stuff, but it's only theory because nobody has found an application. We're here on Mac's NSA grant, to see if an isolated quartz pocket like this might be a sort of natural laboratory for harmonics research."

TEC Squad Room
2008

"Kaki Boyer was just twenty years old when she was recruited," Amy Fuller pointed out. "The best of the best, like all TEC recruits, but you wouldn't know it from her initial NSA evaluation. By almost every criterion, she was an unlikely choice. Too young, too inexperienced, too small . . ."

A segmented screen above the historian's tidy consoles displayed a life-size full-length likeness of a pretty, dark-haired girl barely old enough to be considered a woman. Around the likeness, blocks of letters and numbers outlined vital statistics for a candidate for Time Enforcement Commission service: Mary Katherine Boyer, born 1987 at Williamsburg, Virginia. Height 5'2", weight 116. Parents deceased 2001. No siblings, no close relatives. Court custody as a dependant minor 2001–2004, when a small trust left by her parents kicked in, enabling her to enter college at Broadhurst.

Two degrees in three years with a four-point grade average. Interned with Maryland State Police as a base for her doctorate, distinguished herself as a field officer, and was recruited by TEC.

"Remarkable young woman," Charles Graham commented, scanning the supplementary data. "But I see here that Miss Boyer was considered 'questionable' in her psych evaluations. What's the story on that?"

"P-DAP results," Amy said. "She was screened upon entry into TEC Academy. The overriding characteristics were a very solid moral fiber, a good, inquisitive mind, and a strong score on adaptability. Mary Katherine was one of those rare people who can be just about anybody they want to be, so long as the role matches their sense of values. Logic-derived personality, they used to call it. In our terms it's called autoego, or self-generated identity. All of that went to her credit as a recruit, along with a sort of stubborn, unswerving loyalty and a positive sense of right and wrong.

"At the other end of the P-DAP, though, this recruit showed a strong tendency to become involved in emotional situations. It was difficult for her to distance herself. Sort of an earth-mother type, better for social work than for law enforcement. It was also noted that she was 'culturally isolated,' which simply means she was a lonely kid. And she demonstrated an affinity for 'what's right' more than for 'what's legal.' A natural ethicist. Here again, not exactly the soundest basis for police work. The best of them become saints, the worst of them social activists and politicians.

"Those characteristics raised some flags, but her skill in police work outweighed them. Mary Katherine Boyer became a TEC agent April 22, 2007. She logged two successful field missions, both with Vince Cole as senior partner. Both she and Cole were killed in action—violence attributed to secondary contemporary events—on the second mission . . . or so it says here."

"The 1929 bag-man case," Eugene Matuzek elaborated. "Two rival New York crime cartels had a 'negotiation meeting' at a Bowery speakeasy. It ended in a bloody shoot-out. Our agents and their temporal suspect, a jumper from our own time, were all caught in the middle of it."

"All three deaths verified?" Graham asked.

"Two positive verifications," Amy said. "Both of the

men. News reports and 1929 police records. Cole and the
rogue time jumper were described enough that we know it
was them. There were three women killed, too. None of
them are positively identified. That's how it was, in 1929.
Men were identified in detail. Women were just women—
either wives or otherwise. Anyway, all identifying artifacts came back, in an empty timesled. The official
version is that Kaki Boyer was mortally wounded, but
lived long enough to eliminate the anachronisms. That fits
her ID profile, too. She was stubborn and meticulous."

"And she was still alive a year later," Jack Logan pro-
nounced. "I'm certain she was the 'contemporary' girl I
saw on that rubble lot . . . the one I was watching when I
should have been watching that rookie cop."

Eugene Matuzek gazed at the projected likeness on the
screen and shook his head sadly. "Cute girl," he allowed.
"Cute and pretty. And a good cop, too! I always wondered
what a virus looked like." He turned to Graham. "We've
got a real puzzle on this one, Charlie. Assuming Agent
Boyer survived the 1929 mission, and was on-site at Logan's jump to 1930, we've already put ChronComp on
trace and found a likely intersection point—the town of
Beatrice, Nebraska, in early 1940. A probable match with
a woman named Kaki Sheffield."

"So you're sending an agent to intercept, as we
discussed?"

"That's why I called you," Matuzek said. "We set up a
field mission right after the S and R conference: Ascertain
identity of Agent Mary Katherine Boyer, arrest and return
to TEC present. But the minute we started countdown to
launch, E-warp went crazy. The Dome ran patterns we've

never seen before, and every catastrophe alarm in the place went off."

"A ripple?"

"Not like anything we've ever seen. What does a ripple look like if it doesn't develop somewhen else? The Dome techs think it may have been a major anachronism centered right here, with TEC as epicenter. It blipped off the instant I aborted the launch. ChronComp was no help, either. The vector program wouldn't even come up, and the monitors read 'No access path—eventuality fail-safe.'"

Graham blinked at him. "What does that mean?"

"I haven't the vaguest idea," Matuzek said. "Hemmings is mainlining it direct to S and R, copy to you, but the theorists are just as puzzled as we are." His frown became a scowl. "That egghead-in-chief down there! I asked him for a simple guess, just a clue of some kind, to what happened. Damned smart-ass told me E-warp doesn't want us to go to Beatrice."

Washington, D.C.

"It's got to be tough, being a paradox," Claire Hemmings admitted, pushing bits of some unpronounceable delicacy around with her fork. "I guess it's like setting out to find yourself and there's nobody home."

Beyond big, curved windows the nation's capital paraded past, vistas constantly changing as the restaurant rotated slowly on its two-hundred-foot central shaft. Across the table, Jack Logan turned a cynical gaze toward her, then looked away again. He had hardly touched his food.

Just for a moment, Claire noticed the stubborn set of his

jaw and how it seemed to highlight the hint of sadness in his dark eyes. The suit he wore, a conservative gray with slightly old-fashioned lapels, was brand-new . . . as was everything else he owned. Just one of the myriad problems of a person who suddenly ceases to exist—he didn't have a personal possession of any kind, not even a toothbrush. He didn't have a spare uniform, civilian clothing, or even a change of underwear. He did now, and Claire hadn't decided if she should forgive Eugene Matuzek for saddling her with a paradoxer.

In the past few hours, she had dragged and goaded Logan through a dozen stores and shops, outfitting him for basic, everyday life. Now he wore the attire of any ordinary male denizen of the nation's capital—good, protective coloration.

Civilian garb was necessary if he was to wander around loose outside the confines of TEC. Only rarely was a TEC uniform—or anything related to the Time Enforcement Commission—ever seen in public. TEC was still one of the most closely guarded secrets in the world, and everybody involved intended to keep it that way as long as possible. With the invention of time travel a few years before, through Hans Kleindast's perfection of a means to open and navigate temporal wormholes through the time-stream, Pandora's box had been opened. It could never again be closed, but its chaos potential could be delayed—it was hoped—long enough to create safeguards around it.

Safeguards like the Time Enforcement Commission. A thin blue line of timecops.

And like cops of any kind, they sometimes paid the price for public safety. Jack Logan had paid a horrible price. He had lost his whole world.

He's really a nice-looking man, Claire thought now, wondering for an instant why she found it so easy to be irritated with him. Until a week or so ago, she had never met Jack Logan. But from their very first encounter, on his return from a mission launched in another history, there had been an almost tangible combativeness between them. It was very unprofessional.

"That isn't how it is at all," Logan said now, shaking Claire out of her meditation.

"What?"

"What you said, about looking for oneself and finding no one home. That isn't how it is. I'm quite secure in my own realness. It's the rest of you I wonder about. What kind of world do you have here, where a person can't even order a steak for lunch?"

"A what?" She gawked at him, startled.

"Steak. You know, beef steak? A piece of a cow? It's food, Hemmings. People eat it."

Now, what brought that up? she wondered, feeling the almost automatic annoyance that he brought out in her every time he opened his mouth. "I know what steaks are," she growled. "But I haven't seen one in years. Not since the Balance of Trade treaty with Canada."

"And that's another item for your anomaly scan, Hemmings," Logan said. "What brought on the '85 border embargoes between the U.S. and Canada? Why did the Canucks suddenly decide to call in all their notes, and take payment in meat and grain futures? What happened to the friendship between these countries? And what the hell does my mission to 1930 New York have to do with all of that?" With a glare and a sigh, he turned away again, diving back into his own thoughts. "And why can't a man in your damned history—who never chose to be here—at least have a few bites of grilled sirloin? What kind of a pathetic world builds sky-view restaurants to serve reconstituted soybeans?"

Claire's eyes flashed with a quick, volatile anger. But she held her tongue. It's shock, she thought. He's lost and powerless to undo what's happened. He has a reason for being obnoxious. He's lost everything and doesn't even know why. Slowly, choosing her words with care, she said, "That's a fair question, Logan. What does your being in New York for thirty-seven minutes, seventy-eight years ago, have to do with diplomatic relations between the U.S. and Canada?"

"I don't know," he muttered. "I just don't know."

"Well, then, do you suppose we might stop bickering and find out?"

He turned from the windows, his eyes narrowing with interest. "How?"

"Plain, old-fashioned police work," she suggested. "Why not begin by visiting the scene of the crime?"

"You're crazy, Taffy. This history isn't my history, but it is history for everybody else on earth. We can't tamper with it—"

"Who said anything about tampering? And by the way, that isn't the first time you've called me Taffy." A tiny bell tone sounded, and she raised her hand casually, the onyx ring on her finger brushing her earlobe. She listened for a moment, then stood. "All hands," she said. "A level-three ripple. Ten minutes to briefing."

Versailles, France
June 1935

In the portico off the Coeur de Leon, three dark-coated men emerged from the pillared shadows to surround and contain a stocky, bearded man wearing a fedora and carrying a valise.

They were on him before he realized their presence—three tall, stern men boxing him in, barring his way. "Claude Cartier?" the one before him asked. "You are Claude Cartier, are you not?"

The fedora swiveled this way and that, nervously. "Yes, of course. What do you want of me?"

"We have some questions," the same man said. "Please come with us, quietly."

Flanking him, one of the men gripped his shoulder with fingers like steel bands, while another relieved him of his valise. Herding him among them, almost carrying him, they moved aside to a stone path-wall, and one of them opened the case. Inside were papers—bundles of carbon-copy documents in at least three languages. The dark men glanced at them, then closed the valise.

"Claude Cartier," the one holding his arm said, "I am Inspector Paul Cleriot, Sûreté. I arrest you on charges of espionage for a foreign power. Do you have anything to say?"

"This is an outrage!" Cartier snapped. "Sûreté? And who are these?"

"My witnesses." Cleriot shrugged. "Mr. Johnson represents the United States Embassy, Mr. Serenkov the Union of Soviet Socialist Republics."

He raised a hand in signal. Across the concourse a sleek,

blue Citroën sedan pulled out of its space beside the curb and cut across traffic toward the Rue Pais, slowing to enter the U-turn lane.

"Do you wish to make a statement, M'sieur Cartier?" Cleriot asked again.

Directly above the men, unobserved, the portico ceiling seemed to dissolve in a swirl of coalescing confusion, and a blond woman in white coveralls materialized out of nothingness. She flipped, falling, and landed nimbly on the lip of the path-wall. Before any of the men could react, she crouched, whirled, and doubled Cleriot over with a full-turn kick to the midsection. Without breaking the flow of movement, she dropped the Russian with a hand chop to the nape of the neck, dropped to the paved courtyard, and dodged under the American agent's awkward, startled defense to deliver a knuckle thrust to his larynx.

It was all over in an instant. In the street beyond, passersby were just turning to gape, and the blue Citroën was making its turn around the La Pais monument.

Claude Cartier gawked at the blond woman. Tall and lithe, she seemed to tower over him as she straightened.

"Claude Cartier?" she asked.

"*Oui*—ah, yes," he stammered. "Who—what is this all—"

She stuffed papers back into his valise, closed it, and handed it to him. "They were waiting for you," she said. "There are more in that automobile. Quickly, down those steps, first turn to the left! Go, now!"

Astounded and disoriented, the spy clutched his valise and ran. As he disappeared down the pathway into the Louis Quatorze Gardens, the Citroën skidded to a stop at the curb where three League of Nations security officers lay sprawled and groaning, like fallen debris around a tall, striking blond woman in a white coverall. Before those in the car could pile out, the woman raised a hand to a device on her collar, and disappeared in a mind-numbing swirl of colors—a receding vortex in the empty air.

TEC Squad Room
2008

Jack Logan and Claire Hemmings hurried into the briefing room just as the central screen flashed ThinkTank's vectors on the new ripple:

— LEVEL 3 << —
— O933.007LT —
— ll June 1935 —
— T-Vec Quad 4 —
— 49° N —
— 2° W —

"Versailles, France," Dr. Dale Easter's laser pointer arrowed a chart above the situation monitors. "Rue Pais at the Coeur de Leon. What do we have?"

"One probable." Amy Fuller looked around from her ChronComp direct link. "The arrest of Claude Cartier."

"Sounds familiar." Eugene Matuzek frowned.

Dale Easter squinted through his glasses. "It made headlines a few years later, after the war. Cartier was the one who stole copies of the secret Treaty of Alliance that validated the USSR's position in the League of Nations. A Canadian, probably working with the Croix de Feu. Might have changed World War II if he'd made it. He was caught outside the Coeur de Leon, arrested, and imprisoned for espionage."

"So what's the likely scenario?"

"Somebody using time travel to tamper with history." Easter shrugged. "Eight to five, a jumper going back to thwart the arrest. For a level-three significance, let's assume that if those alliance papers had surfaced in the fascist bloc, we could write off the Allies as a united force against Hitler's Axis gang."

"Best guess, then," Matuzek decided. "We'll intervene on site, target time plus one. Who's up?" He turned. "Logan, suit up. Close intervention is your specialty, according to your evals. You'll partner with—"

"Me!" Hemmings raised a hand. "I'll go."

"That'll work." Matuzek nodded. "Secondary mission— if opportune—observe for on-site anomalies traceable to the 1930 alteration. Is the sublimator capable of dual register, Hemmings?"

"Two eventuality overviews? I can program it in the field, I guess." Claire said. "It'll be random, at best."

"Try it," Easter urged. "The 1935 speed-brief and the brief Logan had on the 1930 mission. I want to give ChronComp all the field data we can. Maybe something will show up in a triangle comparison."

"Two time vectors five years apart, both viewed from whatever the present is upon return?" Claire shrugged. "That ought to be interesting."

"Give me close vectors, Dale," Matuzek ordered. "Launch in five."

Versailles, France
June 1935

Claude Cartier didn't see the waiting men until they had him surrounded. He had expected surveillance. Everyone entering or leaving the Grand Suite of the Louis Quatorze today would be subject to surveillance. But he had not expected confrontation.

The treaty negotiations had concluded a few minutes ago, under blanket security. Cartier had counted on his little scheme—obtaining carbon copies on onion-skin paper direct from the typewriter pool—to give him at least a half hour's head start, enough to deliver the agreements to Comignon and the Croix de Feu, receive his payment, and be gone.

He expected surveillance, and it was there as he stepped out on the portico facing Rue Pais. He spotted the blue Citroën immediately. But he didn't see the big, quiet men closing on him until they were all around him and the one in front held out a big hand to bar his way.

"Claude Cartier?" this one asked. "You are Claude Cartier, are you not?"

Cartier's little goatee bobbed as he glanced this way and that, seeking an escape route. There was none. He felt sweat beginning beneath the band of his fedora. "Yes, of course," he said. "What do you want of me?"

"We have some questions," the man said. "Please come with us, quietly."

Flanking him, one of the men gripped his shoulder with fingers like steel bands, while another relieved him of his valise. Herding him among them, almost carrying him, they moved aside to a stone path-wall, and one of them opened the case.

Cartier was sweating profusely as the men glanced inside—at the bundles of carbon-copy documents. Satisfied, they closed the valise.

"Claude Cartier," the one holding his arm said. "I am Inspector Paul Cleriot, Sûreté. I arrest you on charges of espionage for a foreign power. Do you have anything to say?"

Fear hit Cartier like a fist. He had known, vaguely, that the documents Comignon wanted were important. Now he realized how important. "This is an outrage!" he snapped. "Sûreté? And who are these?"

"My witnesses." Cleriot shrugged. "Mr. Johnson represents the United States Embassy, Mr. Serenkov the Union of Soviet Socialist Republics."

He raised a hand in signal. Across the concourse the blue Citroën sedan pulled out of its space beside the curb and cut across traffic toward the turnaround on Rue Pais.

Beyond the men, on the steps, Cartier saw something indescribable. It looked as though a piece of air came alive, spinning and coalescing, collapsing inward upon itself. Then there were two people there—a tall, dark-haired man and a small honey-haired woman, both clad in close-fitting garments that might have been uniforms had there ever been uniforms such as these.

The Sûreté man was saying something to him. Cartier's mouth snapped shut as he tried to concentrate.

"Do you wish to make a statement, M'sieur Cartier?" Cleriot asked again.

Directly above the men, unobserved, the portico ceiling seemed to dissolve in a swirl of coalescing confusion, and a large, blond woman in white coveralls materialized out of nothingness. She flipped, falling, and landed nimbly on the lip of the path-wall. Before any of the men could react, she crouched, whirled, and doubled Cleriot over with a full-turn kick to the midsection. Without breaking the flow of movement, she dropped the Russian with a hand chop to the nape of the neck, leapt lightly to the paved court-yard, and dodged under the American agent's awkward, startled defense to deliver a knuckle thrust to his larynx.

It was all over in an instant. In the street beyond, passersby were just turning to gape, and the blue Citroën was making its turn around the La Pais monument.

Claude Cartier gawked at the blond woman. Tall and lithe, she seemed to tower over him as she straightened. "Claude Cartier?" she asked.

"*Oui*—ah, yes," he stammered. "Who—what is this all—"

She turned toward the valise. Abruptly, something like a small, fierce tornado hit Claude from the side. His right arm was twisted down, back, and up, imprisoned behind his shoulder. His fedora went flying. His flailing feet barely touching the ground, he was propelled down the wide steps to streetside, just as the Citroën pulled up at the curb.

The car's doors opened, and for an instant Claude Cartier recognized the whirlwind that had caught him. It was the small, honey-haired woman from the steps above.

"Here!" she snapped, thrusting Claude into the car and into the lap of a big, surprised gendarme. In flawless French, she added, "This is Claude Cartier. Four countries want him for espionage, and one for treason."

Up on the portico, the big, blond woman crouched

beside the path-wall, spread muscular arms, and launched herself low and hard at the tall, dark-haired man circling around her. They seemed to collide in midair as the man pivoted, threw himself backward, and propelled her over his head. Even as she recovered her balance, the man grabbed Cartier's valise and threw it—a high, arching pass. "Here, Hemmings!" he shouted. "Catch!"

Cartier's captor picked the valise out of the air and thrust it into the Citroën. "Here is your evidence," she told the gendarmes. "Copies of secret, official government documents."

Up on the portico, the blond woman had launched another attack, this time feinting a tackle that turned into a whirling, low kick. The man's feet flew from under him, and he hit the pavement shoulders first.

The three League of Nations security officers were moving now, two of them on their feet and the third on hands and knees, spitting blood. But the woman ignored them, going again for the uniformed man. Like twisting, feinting tigers they came together, tangled and whirling for a moment. Then the man sailed through the air again, thrown as if from a catapult. As the blond woman moved in for the kill, there was a shout. The agent called Cleriot, recovered now, drew a pistol and pointed it at her. She hesitated, then fingered a device on her collar. In an eye-boggling swirl of coalescence, she disappeared.

From inside the police car, Claude barely saw what happened next. He saw the two dark-uniformed specters meet on the steps, he saw Cleriot's gun waving uncertainly toward first one and then the other of them, and he saw them take hands. Then, like the big woman in white, they disappeared into a vortex of unreality.

Within moments, the area was aswarm with gendarmes and official-looking men in dark coats. Claude Cartier would have slipped away in the confusion, had they given him half a chance. But they didn't. The Versailles gendarmerie was an efficient police force. Once a suspect and evidence were in custody, they did not get lost.

On the pavement beside the car, a pair of plainclothes officials had two of the League men aside. "What happened here?" one of them demanded.

Cleriot shook his head. "We made an arrest. That man, Claude Cartier, a spy. After that, *mon ami*, I have no idea what occurred."

VII

Time Enforcement Commission
2008

A retrieval by timesled is not like a launch, except in terms of sheer physiological terror—the body's natural reaction, despite reassurances by the mind, to unimaginable transition at inconceivable velocities. In other respects, a retrieve is simply the reverse of a launch.

Since a temporal wormhole is an intradimensional phenomenon, there is no distance from one end of it to the other. Thus the time traveler entering retrieval converts instantly from stasis to a velocity of at least 2,994 fps—Q-Velocity—without any apparent shift of inertia, and in that same instant finds himself in the hard grip of pounding deceleration as the sled rams out of oblivion into reality and hurtles toward the launch bay. In time-launch, the traveler prays for velocity. In retrieval, the shocked senses scream for good brakes. That half mile of track, any timecop knows, is the shortest distance in the universe.

"God almighty!" Claire Hemmings breathed as the timesled slid to a halt precisely at its dock. "Do you ever get used to that?"

Canopies lifted and the returnees climbed out of the capsule, fighting the moment of vertigo that always came with the completion of a retrieve. Jack Logan glanced around, almost hopefully, then accepted the fact that the now they had come back to was still the same now from which they had launched. The expressionless scrutiny of Sergeant Glen Malloy told him things hadn't changed. Malloy recognized him, but not from times past.

"Be sure you bring the sublimator wafers," Logan growled at Claire, then turned away to march past bay security and into the sanctum of TEC operations.

Claire stared after him for a moment. "Well, thanks to you, too, Logan," she muttered.

Captain Eugene Matuzek intercepted them on their way to debriefing. "Whatever it was, you fixed it," he said.

"Stella Raines again," Logan said. "Same as before. She wasn't there to steal, or settle a grudge. She was there to change history. We stopped her, but we didn't catch her."

"She tried to interrupt the League of Nations treaties?"

"ThinkTank hit it on the head, this time." Logan started to follow Matuzek into the briefing room, where TEC's top historians and others were already assembled. Then he stopped at the door, stood aside, and let a surprised Claire Hemmings enter ahead of him. "You handled yourself very well in that encounter," he whispered as she passed. "Don't let it go to your head."

When the door was closed, Matuzek told the room, "It was Stella Raines again. She was there, apparently, to thwart the historic arrest of the spy Claude Cartier, and the recovery of stolen treaty documents."

"Obviously, she failed," Dale Easter noted.

"Agents Logan and Hemmings intercepted the attempt and neutralized it," Matuzek said, nodding. "The perpetrator escaped."

Easter fiddled with his glasses. "A critically sensitive moment. The powers were choosing up sides for World War II. Clandestine diplomacy was the order of the day, and espionage had become Europe's industry of choice. If the draft of that Versailles accord had gotten loose, there might never have been an alliance between the U.S. and the USSR. Hitler would still have had his Third Reich, and there would have been war, but Russia might have fallen to the Nazis in the Kiev blitz of 1941."

"Then Josef Stalin would have been hunted down and killed by the Nazis," Bob O'Donnelly added. "Historically, Stella's ultimate target seems to be Stalin."

"It looks that way," Matuzek mused. "First she goes after him through his buddy Roosevelt, then through the Versailles treaties. Your friend Stella doesn't like Stalin very much, does she?"

"Somebody doesn't," Logan muttered. "Somebody wants that old murderer out of history, even if they have to trash history in the process."

They all looked around at him. "What do you mean, 'somebody'?" Easter asked.

Logan turned a conference chair around and straddled it, crossing his arms on its back. His left cheek was starting to swell and darken from one of Stella's strikes. "I know her, remember? I knew her as a TEC trainer, in my own history. If the Stella Raines I knew had a grudge against Josef Stalin, and a time machine at her disposal, she wouldn't be playing games with FDR and the League of Nations. She'd vector directly on Stalin—kill him, or at least beat the bejesus out of him. Either way, she'd break him of sucking eggs."

"You sound like you admire this time jumper, Logan." Matuzek frowned. "Just how well did you know her . . . in that other life?"

"Not like that!" Logan snapped. "Admire her, yes. She's as good as they get. She damned near killed me back there."

"You didn't draw your weapon," Hemmings reminded him.

"I didn't need it." Logan shrugged. "*Damned near killed me* is a figure of speech. I had the situation under control."

"Sure you did!" Claire snorted. "That amazon was throwing you around like a rag doll!"

"Diversion," he said. "My first priority was to preserve history . . . to get those documents out of harm's way."

"So you got them," she pressed. "Looked to me like she still had the upper hand. How about that over-the-shoulder fling? That was—"

"Necessary," Logan said. "I was trying to get her retrieval unit. I missed it, but I did get something else." He raised his closed fist and opened it, letting a little gold amulet dangle there from its chain. "If I'm not mistaken," he said, "this is a Crown Regent coin—Spanish, early 1700s issue. These were common currency at the time of the American Revolution. I think this coin came from that secret treasure I saw in New York in 1930. And unless I miss my guess, if ChronComp can inventory the original coin collection purchased by Alex Porter in Toronto— "

"Portenov," Dale Easter interrupted. "His real name was Aleksei Portenov. He was from Byelorussia—what they used to call a White Russian. He changed the name to Porter when he emigrated to Canada in 1925."

"White Russian." Logan tipped his head. "That's interesting." He tossed the coin on its broken chain across to Matuzek. "Anyway, those coins he bought in 1933 are bound to have been appraised, and maybe photographed and insured. ChronComp should be able to pull up records of some kind. I think we'll find this same coin among that collection."

Oshawa, Ontario, Canada
2008

The man behind the big desk was old—old in years at ninety-three, and far older in some respects. Pale, paper-thin skin stretched over gaunt cheekbones only emphasized the wide, stubborn jawline below. Thick, unruly silver hair over a jutting, Slavic brow matched the heavy eyebrows shading the cold fire of intense, deep-set eyes.

Hunched beneath his blanket, thin and aged, Aleksei Portenov might have looked small, surrounded by the treasures of this, his private sanctum. The room was large and richly appointed, but its furnishings were dimmed by the golden artifacts displayed on lighted shelves all around its walls. There were statues of gold, cups and chalices, golden ornaments from a hundred countries in a dozen ages, and there were coins . . . hundreds and hundreds of gold coins, all carefully displayed.

It was the den of a collector, and Aleksei Portenov did not seem either small or aged here. These were his treasures, and his demeanor drew power from their presence.

Even the big, silent man standing behind his chair—the servant Vassili who was always within reach of him, ready to attend his every need—did not dwarf Aleksei Portenov. Instead, his presence reinforced the dominant power of the old man.

"You have lost your token, Stella *ninichka*," Aleksei Portenov observed now, his cold eyes burrowing into the tall, blond woman who stood submissively before him. "And obviously, you have failed yet again."

"Yes, Aleksei," she said, and nodded. "Again I was interrupted—by people who should not have been there. A different woman, this time, but the same man."

"I am disappointed, *ninichka*," the old man rasped. "I thought there was no man you could not overcome. You have not had such difficulties before."

"No, Aleksei. But this one . . . he seemed to know me! Every technique, every move—it was as though he read my mind. He countered every attack with a parry, every move with its countermove."

The fiery, cold eyes shifted slightly. "Perhaps this man had the same teachers. Your Interpol instructors . . . perhaps that same Zen madman . . ."

"I have encountered this man in the past," Stella reminded him. "In Georgia in 1927, and now again in France, in the year 1935. The martial skills I have mastered—the combination of them—they were unknown then, even in China."

"Is it possible our enemies did not come from those times?" Aleksei Portenov mused. "Could they be time travelers, like yourself?"

"It is the only answer I can imagine," Stella said. "The

weapons they carry, the technology . . . but aside from Am-Can—"

"Am-Can's is not the only timefield in existence," the old man said. "I have always suspected that there are others. The Americans are too firm in their insistence that dimensionality research be limited to 'ethical' boundaries. They are arrogant. Such arrogance arises from secret knowledge." He shifted a bit in his high-back chair, pulling a woolen shawl tighter around his old shoulders. "They have time travel. I am sure of it. And they know that we have it, too. So, these people—this Logan and the others—they are maybe visitors to the past. Likely from our own time, by the tools you described. Could not this Logan have learned where you learned, *ninichka*, if he is of our time?"

She shook her head. "There are skills that did not come from the old Shao-lin, or from Interpol. Skills I developed on my own. This man has those skills, too. There are techniques that only I could have taught him, because they are my own. Yet I have never seen him before, and still he knows."

The shawl shifted as the old man leaned forward. Ancient fingers operated a keyboard, and on the high wall behind the desk a screen came alive. Security-camera views showed a pair of dark-suited men talking to an Am-Can official in the famous Dancing Ice headquarters building in Toronto. The voices were keyed down, and the scene lasted only a moment, then shifted to a magnified view of an official United States government document being handed across a desk.

"Diplomatic rigmarole," Aleksei muttered. "A request for data on an 'unscheduled' activation of Am-Can's dimensional generators. They were fishing, *ninichka*. They had nothing. But from them we know that there is a high-level investigation going on, by the United States government. They suspect that the Roosevelt incident came from Toronto . . . which means they know about our time-launch capability, even if they can't prove it."

The picture on the screen froze, turned, and grew as image-generating computers magnified it further for analysis.

"The United States has a time machine," Aleksei said. "The question is, who has it and for what purpose. Look carefully at this document, Stella *ninichka*. Observe the lower right corner, the symbols there."

Stella stepped closer to the desk, peering upward at the screen. "I see signatures and seals," she said. "All very official."

Again the image grew, until only a corner of the document covered it.

"Bureaucrats will always be bureaucrats," Aleksei Portenov said. "They dearly love acronyms, and revel in misleading design. Do you see the stamped seal beneath the signatures, Stella? A sort of hourglass device within a circle, and the letters *T E C*?"

"It was their insignia," Stella breathed. "The man and at least one of the women—the second one—wore patch shields like that."

She stepped back, returning her gaze to the old man behind the desk. The screen above him flicked off.

"What do we do about them?" she asked.

From a drawer beneath the desk, Aleksei Portenov drew a sleek, laser-sighted handgun of the Schemming design. He laid it on the desk.

"There will be another mission. This time, you must go armed. I ask your indulgence, granddaughter. Assassination is repugnant to all of us. But our cause is in danger now. This time, the mission is to infiltrate and terminate. It may be difficult. The targets are innocent people, not connected with politics. But it must be done."

At the woman's slight hesitation, the old eyes narrowed. "Well, Stella Ilyanova Raines, do you have an objection to my command?"

"No, Aleksei." She picked up the gun and thrust it into the waistband of her white utility suit. "Only—no, Aleksei Portenov. I have no objection. This mission—this assassination—who will it be?"

Again the screen lit up, this time a map of the central United States. A red dot appeared at a spot in southeastern Nebraska.

"The town of Beatrice, in Nebraska," Aleksei said. "Time yet to be selected. Your targets are a husband and wife, who lived there at that time."

"Why?" Stella asked.

"Insurance," the old man said. "The investigation by American officials, into Am-Can. It has some connection with these people, the Sheffields. Events now dictate that a certain trail of events should never have occurred, so you must eliminate that trail. I am sorry that you, yourself, have made this necessary, *ninichka*."

"I?" She stared at him. "How?"

"You lost your token, Stella *ninichka*. Now our enemies have it, and they will find its meaning. But only if they have other events to compare. One other thing: Twice the same man has interfered with our missions. It must not happen again. Next time, *ninichka*, you must kill him."

Damn that fool Dmitri, the old man thought as his granddaughter turned away. This could have been easier done in 1933, when those two Americans were unknown and isolated. But no, Dmitri had to duplicate the timefield and try to steal their money—the same money I paid them for their trove of coins, seventy-five years ago.

For a time, Alex Porter—Aleksei Portenov, onetime hero of the White Russian counterrevolution—worked at his computer console. When finally he had the results he sought, he leaned back while Vassili closed the system. Stella could rest awhile, here in the secluded mansion that was her grandfather's final retreat. Then at a selected hour she would leave by private car for Toronto, to once again use the temporal displacement facility that was Am-Can's greatest experiment.

Opening a locked drawer, Aleksei keyed number codes into a hidden console, opening a direct channel through one of Am-Can's satellites. In Washington, D.C., an old man in a quiet study responded, and in the downlink a Toronto computer verified his voiceprint, palm impression, and retinal scan.

"Yuri," Aleksei Portenov said. "On six-six-two you will find a document. Study and erase. Note at lower right, the acronym *TEC*. Full resource on this, please. What is TEC? Where is TEC? Who is TEC? Full resource, Yuri. Report directly to me and only to me."

Beatrice, Nebraska
October 1971

"I've never seen anything like it, Mom." Jimmy Sheffield grinned. "They're listening to a quartz cavern out there, and it's showing them things you wouldn't believe!"

Kaki pushed back her graying hair and favored her son with a quizzical, amused glance. "I might," she said. "Try me."

Bright, morning sunlight gloried through the chiffon curtains at the bay windows, and the chords of a new, experimental melody drifted from the study where Harry Sheffield was doing things with piano and synthesizer—sound patterns that hadn't been done before. Jimmy stood, stretched his arms, and rolled his shoulders, then stepped across to the counter where a percolator was tapering down from brew.

He's tall, Kaki mused. Tall like his father, and with the same restless, bubbling dreamer's energy about him.

Jimmy poured two cups and returned to the nook. "I've signed on for a stint with them," he said. "They want me to make magic out of their magic."

Children's voices drifted from the upstairs hall, where Tammy was grooming the rug rats into a semblance of propriety. "Magic?" Kaki asked.

"Yeah, sort of. You see, they've put together a team. Mac Wainwright's the straw boss, with an NSA grant. They're doing research on Cyrus Infeld's theories—perpetual resonance, dimensional eventuality, stuff like that. That quartz pocket at Paxton Peak is sort of a natural laboratory for harmonic testing."

"I follow about 20 percent of that." Kaki smiled. "But I'm with you so far. When will you report in?"

"Thursday. Tammy wants to stop over in Denver for a shopping binge, before we consign ourselves to a wilderness winter. So we'll leave tomorrow." He glanced out the window, then leaned for a better look. "Who's the blond Valkyrie across the street?"

Kaki glanced out. In a driveway across the quiet street, a tall, blond woman stood. Her back was to them, but even from behind she was a striking figure in white slacks and sweater.

"Oh, I guess that's the woman Jane Ryan mentioned. A Canadian woman who might rent their garage apartment. I guess she's made up her mind."

She went back to her polishing, humming quietly as Harry's latest harmonies swelled from the study.

"Well, she'll do wonders for the neighborhood," Jimmy said, still at the window. "That's a good-looking woman. In fact, that's almost two good-looking women."

"She does look tall, doesn't she?" Kaki put away a plate. "Jane thinks she's an athlete of some kind, or used to be. I really haven't met her. I just saw her helping Jane move some crates of books. She handled them like they were nothing. I think Jane said her name is Stella. If she decides to take the apartment, we'll get better acquainted. What, exactly, does perpetual resonance mean?"

Jimmy hesitated, framing his response. With his mother, it was always hard to tell whether she was curious about a new thing or simply comparing semantics—as though she knew all about the technology but didn't know what it was called. He decided to take the question at face value. "I'll show you," he said.

He walked into the family room, where a shiny new videocassette recorder rested on a shelf beside the equally new color television set. A handful of VCR tapes lay there, and he picked one up and carried it back to the breakfast nook.

"It's like this," he said. "A roll of magnetic tape electronically imprinted by a sequence of stimuli—in this case, pictures and sounds translated into magnetic impulse. That's an analogy. We're looking at—well, at who knows what, imprinted by a sequence of stimuli we don't really understand, in a medium that goes beyond our theories of impulse."

"Got ya." Kaki nodded. "Sequential probability, a perpetual record of occurrence, with the elemental dimensions as the matrix. Eventuality-wave resonance. The perpetual record of the time line."

Dr. James Henry Sheffield gawked at his mother. "What?"

"If you want a tag for it," she said, "call it E-warp. That's quite a leap from music theory, Jimmy. Where do you fit in?"

In the background, piano and synthesizer music swelled in a breathtaking, bittersweet crescendo. They listened, rapt, and Jimmy breathed, "My God, that's beautiful. What does he call it?"

"He doesn't call it anything." Kaki shrugged. "It's for a screenplay. They'll parcel it out to a dozen people who'll mush it up and put their names on it. It's the market these days. Big music only sells in little pieces. What part of the E-warp project is yours, Jimmy?"

"Interpretation, I guess. Charlie Wang has come up with a harmonic sensor that picks up resonances that aren't there, and Mac Wainwright has tracked the Infeld theories into a dimensionality problem. Omer Harrison's working with crystalline harmonics, Dave Spivy has a set of equations that seem to span the energy-matter gap, and Ito Nogura's trying to apply quantum mechanics to a stable matrix. They sort of expect me to put all the pieces together and make a picture out of it."

"Make magic out of magic." Kaki nodded. "Can you do it?"

"I'm going to give it a shot. What did you call that string of notions you tossed out there, Mom? E-warp? Not bad. Maybe I'll name their project for them."

"You might as well." Kaki smiled. "Somebody has to."

Outside, on the leaf-blown lawn, Stella Raines turned and listened as the mighty chords and haunting melody of Harry Sheffield's latest creation echoed from the Sheffield house. Beautiful, she thought. Magnificent! So that's how it sounded before Hollywood chopped it up and sugar-coated it!

She would kill Harry Sheffield, soon. He and his bright-eyed little wife, Kaki. It would take a few days, to set it up to attract no attention. But when it was ready, she would do it. She would never break her vow to her grandfather.

She wouldn't like it, though. It was the way of the world that great causes take precedence over the lives of innocent people, but it was a shame that a man who made such music must die in the cause of a justice that would be seven decades in coming.

TEC Headquarters
2008

"What the hell is this, Hemmings?" Eugene Matuzek slapped a document down on his desk and glared at TEC's surprised systems analyst, who had just arrived in his office.

Claire Hemmings blinked, cocked her head to glance at the document on the desk, then shrugged. "Research mission requisition," she said. "From S and R. I requested it. Is something wrong?"

Matuzek's frown was thunderous. "Are you crazy, Hemmings? This is a requisition for a time-launch to specific vectors on South Birney Street, New York City, insertion at twelve hundred hours on May 12, 1930!"

"Yes, I know," Claire assured him. "An hour ahead of that branch-history mission of Logan's. A lot happened on that mission, and we don't know what it was. I think we ought to go back and take a look."

"Hemmings, do you realize the risks of repeat insertions at the same locale in the same day, much less the same hour?"

"Fairly minimal—" Claire spread her hands. "—assuming the second team takes every precaution to avoid contact with the first."

"Or contact with anyone who might have contact with the first team," Matuzek snapped. "Or even being seen by anybody who might happen to mention to anybody else on that day that they saw some people materialize out of thin air. God! The implications of a dual probe are textbook stuff, Hemmings! And to top it off, you suggest that Jack Logan be a member of the observation team, which means that one of the people he's observing is himself, in another life . . . before he lost that other life."

"I don't think it's all that much of a risk, Captain," Claire argued. "Logan's the best choice, because he's the only one who might know what to look for. He was there. I'd be the other team member, and you could make me the team leader—"

Matuzek lowered his head over his crossed arms, like a man praying for patience. Then he looked up again. "Have you gone dense, Hemmings? Jack Logan is a good cop. A first-rate timecop. But, God, girl, he's only human! Right there, right then, is where he lost his whole world. Don't you think he wants it back? Don't you think there might be a thousand ways he could . . . readjust the history that went askew at that point? Just the slightest little nudge, it might not even be a conscious thing, and zap! There goes our history, right down the drain. Jack said it himself, Hemmings—this world he came back to may not be his world, but it's the only world everybody else in it has got!"

"I—I think it's worth a try," Claire pursued, less sure now. "I don't think Jack Logan would— "

"No," the TEC captain said emphatically. "No! Now you take your S and R requisition and make it disappear, and don't even think about it again! That's an order!"

Claire straightened to attention, snapped an angry salute, and turned to the door. But with her hand on the latch, she turned back. "Captain, if you won't let Logan work on his own problem, then put him to work on something else. Give him something to do besides mope around waiting for a ripple. The man is driving me crazy!"

VIII

Washington, D.C.
2008

Off duty and with time on his hands, Jack Logan prowled the streets around the Capital Mall, sightseeing like a tourist in a city thoroughly familiar to him . . . but not quite. Seventy-eight years of history were not exactly the seventy-eight years he knew, and there were changes. A certain skyline was not exactly as it had been, a park had slightly different amenities, a highway loop was subtly different, there was an apartment building where a hotel had been . . .

History was like marbles on a plate, a TEC theorist had explained once. Let just one marble roll, and it will move another, and that yet another. Drop the same marbles onto the same plate a thousand times, and each time you'll have a plateful of marbles, but never quite the same as any other version of the same thing.

"And all for want of a nail," Logan mused darkly, feeling the lingering loneliness of a man who, historically, did not exist—had never existed—in this reality around him. He took the tube to Lincoln Heights and back, spent a few hours walking around Georgetown, and had a discouraging meal at a deli specializing in meat-substitute sausages.

The deli was just across the street from his third-floor rented room, and he had seen it from the window yesterday, when he moved in. He thought about that, and scowled. Yesterday it had not been a deli. Yesterday it had been a kolache shop . . . hadn't it? The marbles seemed always to be moving.

He wondered if nonexistence heightened a person's awareness of progressive alteration. An unstable history, Dale Easter had suggested. This reality certainly was more volatile than the one he remembered, as though this one just wasn't quite real enough to stabilize itself.

"But what did I have to do with that?" he asked himself for the thousandth time, going back over—and over and over—every second of that mission to the Manhattan of 1930. He had revisited the memory so many times these past days, including an unpleasant stimulated recall session with the S and R crowd and their toys, that the whole episode remained as vivid as recall can be.

It had started with a point-four ripple on the Dome of History. Not really a big anachronism, but still a definite alteration of history. ThinkTank had equated epicenter with a collection of significant historical events—the finding of the Lord North Treason Papers from Revolutionary times, a labor riot at a construction site, an entire matrix of concurrent events. But no one event had surfaced as an exact match for the ripple.

Logan had been assigned and had launched to the twelfth of May, 1930, on Lower Manhattan Island. He recalled Hemmings sniping at him about the sublimator—a piece of technological wizardry that he despised on general principles—and Easter and O'Donnelly playing word games with *persnickety* and *finicky*, and he recalled the launch. One always remembers a time-launch . . . and an insertion.

There had been a sort of desultory, widespread riot going on—angry civilians prowling here and there over a large, rubble-mounded construction site, and a lot of police working in squads to contain the situation.

He recalled materializing five feet above ground level—temporal vectoring was its usual faulty self—and falling into an excavation pit. He fell, and collided with a rosy-cheeked young cop who was already there. And then Logan had discovered the gold—a wide, mounded pile of bright coins glistening through the dirt at the bottom of the excavation. The young cop had seen the coins, too, which was why he was in the pit.

Old coins. Historic coins. Yet there was no reference to any gold coins in the historical appraisal offered by ChronComp.

The young policeman had been nervous and alert. A good cop, obviously, but still just a rookie. Logan had known that he wasn't satisfied with Logan's assurance that he, too, was a policeman. He had known that the situation was volatile. But there had been an instant's distraction—a young woman out on the construction site where no young woman should be.

And that young woman had been someone he later recognized—Kaki Boyer, a TEC agent listed as KILD.

Logan had been distracted, and the young cop had seized the advantage. Logan could still feel the decisive impact of his nightstick, even the solid weight of him as he wrist-pinned the timecop. Logan's only recourse was to retrieve back to his own time.

But it wasn't his time anymore. He no longer existed! And in this world he had returned to, history was not as stable as in the world he had left.

Again the memories came full circle, and again there was something missing.

"What do I have to do with that?" he asked himself, concentrating fiercely. "What happened that cancelled my life and made all these other changes? What does the one have to do with the other?"

And a thought struck him, between chews of pasty soy-sausage: Nothing! There is no relationship between what happened to my history, and what happened to world history. It wasn't one thing that occurred, there in south Manhattan on May 12, 1930. It was two! Simultaneous, but unrelated.

And that thought only complicated questions that had no answers. What should have been a simple jump had resulted in various changes in history, but what had caused the changes? The gold coins that were there but weren't found? The cop he had tangled with? Maybe even himself, somehow?

And finally: What had E-warp sensed, that caused the ripple on the Dome? Had there been a rogue time jumper there that he had not seen? What was changed? And what in God's name was a missing-presumed-dead TEC agent doing among the time-line inhabitants of 1930?

Frustrated, his head aching with intense concentration, Logan wandered over into the West Mall area and found a movie theater. The place was at least twenty years old, a holdover from the blockbuster film days of the nineties, and most of the features were time-honored classics. *The Amityville Horror* shared billing with *The Color Purple* and *Yentl*. There was *The Godfather*, *Independence Day*, *Tree of Hearts*, and *One Flew Over the Cuckoo's Nest*—twenty-one screens of the accumulated output of that weird subculture known as Hollywood, which for three generations had lived in its own shadow, consumed its own dreams, and managed, somehow, to spit out profitable, popular entertainments captured on 35-millimeter film.

Logan had seen every film offered. Everybody had seen them, years ago. But he bought a ticket for the one he remembered most fondly—the grandest and last of the big-score musicals, *Song of Eterne*.

For nearly three hours it passed his time, and he found it was best when he closed his eyes. The musical score was tantalizing, bordering on magnificent. Bits and pieces of mastery, Logan thought, served à la carte.

He slept, the sounds soothing him, and awakened to see the final titles rolling. And there, far down in the credits, was a little acknowledgement: Musical score suggested by the works of Harry Sheffield. Not the primary author of anything, but the source of it all!

Sheffield. The name had emerged in recent investigations within TEC. Sheffield the musician. Kaki Boyer's Harry Sheffield?

Logan left the theater, flagged a cruise-cab, and headed for TEC. He wanted some serious time with ChronComp's omnivorous data files.

The world's best-kept secret, like most great secrets of the twenty-first century, was concealed within the obvious. Few people in the year 2008 had any inkling that time travel—the intentional passage of people and things to times and places in the past—had become a practical reality. The technology behind dimensional transference was public knowledge, and had been for decades. But its practical principles were single sand grains within mountains of scientific theory far too vast for any human brain to sift.

Everybody knew about the mountains. Some even knew the intricacies of quantum physics that were their trace elements. But only a handful had access to the technology that had produced the wormhole principle and the timefield insertion capability developed by Dr. Hans Kleindast.

In much the same way, the Time Enforcement Commission existed within the huge structure of the federal government, visible to the public only as an acronym—one of tens of thousands of vague, alphabet-soup subagencies: the TEC. Its documentation was a few faceless documents hidden in a maze within a maze. It was just one of hundreds of secret projects within the untrackable web of NSA's Black Ops division, headed by that legendary wizard of the covert, Charles Graham.

And as with all of Graham's pet projects, every documentary path toward the existence of TEC was guarded by computer flags, alarms, and trip wires.

Thus when discreet inquiries were made—persons outside the circle of privilege expressing curiosity about "something called TEC"—the matter came directly to Graham's attention. Within hours, the source of the inquiries was identified.

"We've hooked a fish, in our investigation of Am-Can,"

Graham confided to Captain Eugene Matuzek. "My people dangled a glimpse of the TEC logo, and somebody took the bait. His name is Yuri Gregorievich Raskin. Thirty years ago he was a wheelhorse in the Dosvestia movement—a sort of White Russian Zionist underground based in the U.K. Fanatics, mostly, but they did a lot to undermine the old USSR."

"I've heard of Dosvestia." Matuzek nodded at the comlink screen and the famous face on it. "When I was a kid. I didn't know they were still around, though. Their purpose disappeared when Communism collapsed, didn't it? There isn't any USSR anymore."

"Old grudges die hard," Graham said. "But Yuri Raskin's a little fish. I want the big one, the one who sent Yuri to inquire about TEC. So I need bigger bait."

"Tell me what you need." Matuzek shrugged.

"I want to use the paradoxer. Logan. I want to dangle him. He's the agent that jumper called Stella encountered. So whoever's using Am-Can to skew history, they know him. She's seen him, and I'm sure she's described him, so we won't have to create a cover for him. Gene, I want to let Yuri Raskin know who Logan is. Let's throw him out and see who bites."

"You want to paint a bull's-eye on one of my people, Charles?"

"Exactly. He's an ideal choice. They can't get to his family; they can't go back and change his history. They can't get to his past, because he doesn't have one. They'll have to go at him head-on. He'll be the only lead they have to TEC. He'll be a target, if he's willing and you agree."

"And he's supposed to stand around waiting for somebody to track him down and shoot him? Logan's not the passive type, Charles."

"Then assign him this case. Give him a material witness warrant for Stella Raines and whoever's behind her. Turn him loose on it, with authority and department resources. I'll provide the data and deputize him under Secret Service, Official Secrets authority. Just warn him that the bad guys are going to recognize him, because we'll see to it that they do."

Jack Logan appeared in the squad room at 7 A.M.—rumpled, unshaven, and disheveled. He clocked in and headed for the captain's office.

"I want you to look at these," he told Matuzek, tossing a pair of compact wafers onto his desk. "Sequences of events from the 1930 mission. Every likely cause-and-effect sequence I can come up with. ChronComp verifies that it's highly unlikely that the same anachronism that changed my history also caused all the other changes. I've spent the night with ChronComp, coming up with these, but they prove that at least two separate, unrelated events occurred at almost exactly the same time."

Matuzek glanced at the CWs, then looked up at Logan, sadly. "We already know that, Jack. ThinkTank has generated the same scenarios."

"Well?"

"Well, what? So now we know that there were multiple alterations in history on May12, 1930. So what difference does it make? There's nothing we can do about it. The alterations were made, and not reversed. So now they're history, Jack."

"We could go back and look," Logan pressed. "Dammit, Gene—"

"Let it go, Jack. You're playing with matches. We aren't going to make a second insertion into the same time and place, and that's it. It's too risky, even if—"

"Even if, what?" Logan flared, then sighed. "Even if it's somebody else who goes, right? Somebody you could trust?"

"I didn't mean that."

"Yes, you did. I know the procedure manual, too, Captain. I helped you write some of it . . . back in that other life. 'Considering the natural, human desire to correct mistakes, the placement of any anachronistic individual at the scene of his anachronism would create an unstable situation in which the risk outweighs the reward.' That's what it says, isn't it?"

Matuzek gazed at him. "Not the exact words, but that's the gist of it. You really did participate in the procedures conferences, didn't you!"

"I told you I did."

"Well, then you know the risks. I'm sorry, Jack. It's out of the question. 1930 happened, and it's past. Whatever occurred back there is history now, and we don't change history. Anyway, I have an assignment for you, if you want to volunteer. Special project status, contemporary. Somebody is trying to penetrate TEC, and your old friend Stella is involved in it. This is high-risk, ground-zero stuff, Jack. Not timecop work, just present-day police work. Your authority will be special projects, Secret Service."

Logan slumped tiredly, accepting the inevitable. Then he straightened himself. "Okay," he said. "I'll volunteer. What's the situation?"

"It's a fishing expedition," Matuzek said. "You'll be the bait."

Oshawa, Ontario

Aleksei Portenov pulled the comforter tighter around his ancient frame and gazed at the monitors on his wall. Once again, as in the old days, Yuri Raskin had managed to piece a few harmless inquiries into a vital intelligence. He didn't know what TEC meant, or why there were U.S. federal agents probing into the operations of Am-Can, but he had found a lead. The individual displayed on the monitor was a tall, athletic-looking man in his thirties, and his name was Jack Logan.

From Yuri's investigations, Portenov knew that this Logan was somehow connected with the inquiries into Am-Can. And he knew where to find him. Just yesterday, the man had booked a suite at the Watergate and had gone from there to the Department of State, where he had spent an hour and twenty minutes in conference with an official of historical archives. They had accessed seventy-year-old intelligence reports dealing with the day-to-day movements of the Russian Communist dictator, Josef Stalin, in the 1930s.

A sense of urgency drove Portenov as he coded a message into Am-Can's sealed comlink—a message to some very efficient and very expensive people that even Yuri didn't know about.

When the message was acknowledged, Aleksei Portenov wagged an imperious finger, and the silent, omnipresent Vassili appeared at his side.

"It is time for my bath, Vassili," he said.

The big man nodded a curt bow and stepped around behind the chair. Gently but efficiently he disconnected the old man's catheters and reconnected them to a portable rack on the back of the chair. Then he wheeled him from the room.

Aleksei ignored the big man's silent ministrations, thinking instead about the impending arrival of a live TEC agent.

"Vassili," he commanded, "tell Grigor to go to the Eaton warehouse and take the doctor with him. He will receive instructions there."

He wished that his granddaughter, Stella Raines, could be on hand when Jack Logan was delivered to the sealed warehouse off Eaton Center in Toronto. Stella had actually encountered the man, on two missions. Her knowledge might be useful in prying information out of the reluctant "guest." But Stella was on another time mission now and would not return to the present until her assignment was done.

It didn't matter, though. Aleksei had others to do his bidding. A little time with Grigor, he thought, and this Jack Logan would be begging to tell him everything he knew about TEC and about why U.S. officials might meddle with Dosvestia's long-awaited destiny.

Washington, D.C.

"God, I hate this part," Jack Logan muttered—as much to himself as to the listeners—as he approached the door to his rented suite at the Watergate Hotel. They would be inside by now, the ones waiting to accost him. The doorway's lock was still locked, and the tiny, mercury-circuit telltale on its hinge had not sent its alarm. But the sensors under the carpet had told their story. The room had been penetrated from a utility duct, and there were people inside, waiting for him.

They were good at what they did, and it would be over in a hurry. It was what he had waited for—for two days now, since his identity was leaked by NSA.

But that didn't make it any easier to open that door.

Mentally, Logan checked his preparations—the fake papers in his wallet, the CW recorder concealed in his belt, and the little transponder that rested like a miniaturized hearing aid in his ear.

"I'm going in," he muttered, not moving his lips, and the transponder in his ear responded with a "Good luck, Jack," that only he could hear.

Logan hesitated, sensing the tiny, tender spot in the palm of his left hand. Then he took a deep breath, keyed the thumb-scan on the apartment door, and stepped into whatever came next.

"Make it look good, Logan," the transponder whispered, this time with a feminine voice.

The words were unnecessary. As strong arms closed around his arms and a heavy, dark sack descended over his head, Logan's reflexes took over. He dropped, becoming dead weight in the grip of the big man behind him, and at the same time doubled both legs and lashed out forward. The one with the sack flew backward across the room and caromed off a closet door frame. In the same flow of motion, Logan twisted his body, heaved back, and braced his feet on the carpeted floor.

When he came upright, the assailant behind him pitched over his head, upside down, and thudded to the floor behind him.

Logan spun, crouched to grapple, and something hard and heavy collided with his skull from one side. He staggered, then fell as his feet were pinned and someone slugged him again. Half-conscious, he struggled to rise, but there were men on top of him. His arms were grasped, pulled back cruelly, and secured with a come-along. A heave, and his hands and feet were snugged into a snare-tie behind him. Hard fingers turned his head this way and that, grinding his face into the carpet, and he felt the transponder ripped from his ear.

Then the sack was over his head again, stifling him. Distantly he heard a muffled click and felt the sting of a hypodermic injection between his shoulder blades. Reality spun and darkness descended on the wry, unspoken question: Did that look good enough, Hemmings?

With his last shred of will, Jack Logan clenched his left fist, middle finger first, activating the subdermal device implanted in his palm—a tiny, powerful ELF transmitter no larger than a grain of table salt. The extremely low frequency range was almost impossible to detect, for the same reason that its use as a broadcast range was virtually useless: Its pulse was so long and so slow that it might take hours to transmit a single, simple bit of data. ELF's only practical characteristic was that its impulses would go anywhere, through anything, and distance meant nothing to it. They would find the ear transponder and the CW recorder. They would find the fake papers. They would find everything . . . except, maybe, the ELF.

Bright light and confusion buffeted him as Logan swam

upward through the darkness of near-death and back into the world of consciousness. His head ached abominably, his returning nerve senses were bright bursts of pain, and he clenched his eyes closed to try to shut out the punishing, tormenting light.

"He's coming around, Grigor," a voice said.

Hard thumbs pushed back his eyelids, and blinding flashes of light played across his distended pupils. Logan tried to turn his head away, but it wouldn't move. A strap tightened across his forehead, and punishing bonds ground into his wrists and ankles. He was strapped down, spread-eagle on his back, and now a face swam into view—a wide, heavy-featured face framed by close-cropped gray hair.

The face leered at him—a kindly, jovial old man's face seamed with good-natured creases and wrinkles softened by a silver burr of close-cut whiskers. Santa Claus, Logan's sluggish mind thought. Then he focused on hard blue eyes beneath silvery brows, and changed his mind. There was no hint of joviality in those eyes. They were as cold and remote as winter skies.

"Good morning, Mr. Logan," the man said. "So glad to have you with us today. I expect you'll be telling us all about yourself in a few minutes." The face turned away and the same voice, harsh and cold now, said, "This subject is still partially anesthetized. Revive him."

A hypodermic gun clicked, and Logan felt its sting. Then hot, lancing pain shot through his shoulders, along his arms, and spread like fire through his torso and down his legs. He writhed and gasped, willing it away, and came fully awake.

"That's better." The gray-whiskered man nodded, peering into his eyes. "Now I believe we can begin. Mr. Logan, what is TEC?"

Beyond the glaring lights, at a distance, were dark, geometrical forms—girders and rafters, supporting a roof. The sound of emptiness surrounded the lighted area, and he knew he was in a large, enclosed building like a warehouse. Again he strained at his bonds, but they didn't give at all.

"Come, come, Mr. Logan," the old man urged him. "You're wasting my time. You will answer all my questions, you know. One way or another. One more time, now. What is TEC? What do those letters mean?"

"Would you believe *Thomas Edward Coleman*?" Logan rasped. "Or maybe *Take Extra Care*?"

An angry hand swung into view, striking downward to slap him across the face. With his head held immobile the blow stunned him for an instant. Then he felt warm blood running from his nose, down his cheek. The old blue eyes turned away, and the man said, "Show him, doctor. But just a little."

Logan couldn't see the other man, the one called doctor, but abruptly a searing pain lanced through him, jolting him, bending him upright like a drawn bow—a spasm, a convulsion of torment that took his breath away. It subsided after a moment, and gradually Logan regained control of his breathing. He didn't know whether he had screamed or not. The momentary pain had been so intense that he had been blind and deaf.

Moments passed, then the bewhiskered face was over him again, smiling serenely. "That was just a sample, Mr. Logan. The doctor is very good with his toys. He learned his craft from the NKVD itself. The electric arc is such a simple device, though. He much prefers the more permanent disfigurements. It is how he deals with his own mutilation. Now, it really is time for you to talk to me, before I turn him loose. What is TEC?"

Logan clenched his jaws shut, tried to squirm, tried to find a weakness in the unrelenting bonds, and the cold voice said, "Very well, Mr. Logan. Go ahead, doctor. But carefully. Leave at least enough of him to give me answers to my questions."

Logan braced himself, but instead of the excruciating pain he expected, there was a gunshot, followed by the harsh, high-pitched command, "Stand very still, you icy bastard! Don't even twitch!"

Hands were at his bonds, then, freeing his straps, and Logan sighed his relief. "It's about time you showed up, Hemmings. What kept you?"

"Wonder I got here at all," Claire Hemmings said, standing over him with a handgun trained on someone beyond. "That jolt they gave you burned out your ELF. We had to set the vectors by dead reckoning."

"You didn't launch until I was already being tortured?"

"Launch to where? Did you ever try to get quick focus on an ELF signal? By the time ChronComp had a fix, the signal was gone. We didn't know your situation, so we gave it twelve hours' leeway."

Logan sat up, aching all over. "Great!" he muttered. "You've been here for twelve hours! I went through all this, and here you've been here the whole time . . . twelve hours?" He glared at her. "Why didn't you interrupt these sadists an hour ago, if you had all that free time?"

"I used the time to look around." She returned the glare, but the gun in her hand never wiggled. Logan knew it was pointed at Santa Claus. "Do you know where we are, Logan? We're in Toronto, Ontario. In Canada. They brought you up here in a packing crate, as part of a load of furniture. This building is a closed shipping warehouse, but it's just a cover. There are roll-away stairs, and a trap that leads to a research complex the size of the Superdome. Most of it's underground. By the way, O'Donnelly got a positive match on that old coin you got off Stella Raines. It's definitely one of the coins Alex Porter bought in 1933, right here in Toronto."

"Am-Can," Logan breathed, rubbing his sore wrists. "This is an Am-Can facility?"

"Not just a facility," Claire said. "This place is Am-Can. It's their headquarters. It's no wonder our people never knew exactly where Am-Can based its operations. There's a big shopping mall above it, and a couple of high-rise office buildings. Porter Tower connects, where the Am-Can offices are, but everything good's underground. There's even a timefield generator, and a sled track that must be nearly a mile long! I guess it was a subway tunnel, once."

"Marvelous," Logan growled. "And I guess you got so caught up in it all that you forgot why you were here? I could have used a more timely rescue, Hemmings. They were killing me."

"Oh, they weren't, either," Claire sneered. "Just a little electrical charge. I didn't want to step in too early. The goons that snatched you and brought you up here were still around, until a few minutes ago. Too iffy, Logan. Too much chance of a botched collar."

Shaking his head, Logan looked around. The table he had been strapped to was a hospital gurney. Next to it, a metal cabinet held instruments that would have made Torquemada drool. A few feet away, the old man with the silvery whiskers stood scowling, his hands above his head. And just beyond the instrument cabinet, a figure sat hunched in a mechanized wheelchair, blood soaking the front of his white hospital frock. The tool dangling from his dead fingers was a high-speed crafting tool, fitted with a one-inch circular saw.

"Of course, I guess I did cut it a little fine," Claire admitted. "Another few seconds and you'd have started losing some semiessential body parts."

Logan realized for the first time that he had been stripped. He was nearly naked, and he wrapped a sheet around his waist. Then, on slightly shaky legs and staying out of Claire's line of fire, he walked to where the whiskered man stood. Though sturdy and powerfully built, the old man looked even older now, deep brow shadows shading his cold, fanatical blue eyes. Logan paced angrily halfway around him, bent to examine the dead man in the wheelchair, and straightened, looking bleak. The dead man had no legs.

"Stalin's work," Grigor said, behind him. "Even after the beast was gone, his methods went on. The doctor had the misfortune to displease the NKVD. When they released him, he had lost his legs and his mind."

Logan spun around, glaring down at the whiskered man. "So somebody brought him to Canada," he growled. "Somebody found work for him here, and you know who that somebody was."

Still staying out of Claire's line of fire, Logan patted down the old man, then grabbed a handful of coat collar, and dragged him to the strap-down gurney. "All right, Grigor," he said. "Now it's time for you to talk to me."

IX

Toronto, Ontario
2008

"You wouldn't really have done that, would you?" Claire demanded as the two timecops emerged from a long-unused freight shaft into a vast, echoing maze of subterranean passages—the forgotten fringes of a virtual underground city beneath a city. Claire led the way, using a palm-scan to follow the trail of her earlier explorations.

"Done what?" Logan asked, his alert gaze flicking here and there, getting his bearings.

"You wouldn't really have . . . well . . . started amputating parts of Grigor. I mean . . . really, Logan? That poor old man!"

"Yeah, I know." Logan shrugged. "He reminded you of Santa Claus. Forget it, Hemmings. That fanatic wasn't Santa Claus. Grigor Soloviev was a lot closer to the Marquis de Sade than to Saint Nick. He only understood one kind of persuasion, and I used it. It worked. We got what we could from him."

"Yeah." She nodded. "And you scared him to death . . . literally. Those spasms—that was a massive stroke that hit him. Cerebral hemorrhage, triggered by dire threats! You're an animal, Logan. Do you know that?"

"I know that a person who believes in torture is afraid of being tortured. He thought I'd start cutting. People expect other people to do what they would do. If that apoplexed that old monster to death, that was his problem, not mine. Where do all these corridors go?"

"They go all over. The walls are the pillars and foundations of Eaton Center, one of the biggest shopping malls in North America—great cover for a secret scientific base. We're in the back part of the maze here. Forgotten territory, except for the project engineers and maybe the provincial building inspection division."

They went on, following the scan, their only light the dim radiance of occasional incandescent panels and Claire's little torch. Both of them were in uniform now, the distinctive dark flak cloth of TEC agents. Claire flashed her light on a metal panel between prestressed concrete pillars. There were wiring and piping diagrams posted beside the door, and a sign: EATON CENTER WEST MAINTENANCE SECTOR—NO UNAUTHORIZED ADMITTANCE.

"This goes to the subbasement of the mall," Claire said. "Low security. I froze the lock earlier."

She pulled the trap open, peered beyond, then stepped through. Jack followed, into a maintenance corridor. Here there were vinyl floors and lights, and the smell of cleaning supplies. Fifty yards along, the corridor turned and they found themselves in the great belly of a modern commercial center. Huge furnaces were ranked side by side, their ductwork spanning outward along ceiling paths. Waste disposal systems, electrical conduits, water and plumbing systems—all the necessities of life under a vast

roof were here, circling a central chamber where maintenance people went about their chores while computer
banks in a glass-enclosed central island ran the systems
that supported the mall above.

Claire pointed at a gap between ranked blowers. "There's
a security corridor there, Logan. Am-Can's territory begins just beyond."

"You've penetrated it?"

"Far enough to see that there's another, tighter ring of
security beyond the open labs. Real high-tech stuff. That's
where the time-travel operation is."

"And you've seen it?"

"I had a pretty good look at it. The security is tight, but
they use the same air ducts as the rest of the complex. I
scanned the whole operation." She touched a small utility
pouch at her waist, beneath her utility belt. "Our techs are
going to be interested in these wafers. Am-Can's time
technology is practically identical to TEC's, right down to
the tachyon drives on the timesled. It's a carbon copy,
adapted to an old subway system. Somebody's going to
have some tall explaining to do."

"I want to see it," Logan said.

"Okay, it's your show at this point, Logan. Just what are
we looking for?"

"Answers," Logan growled. "Grigor told us who's behind these assaults on history—"

"Yeah, if you want to believe that Alex Porter is still
alive. That was about all I got. Russian's one of your languages, not mine."

"Alex Porter." Logan nodded. "The man behind Am-
Can. Only his name wasn't always Porter. He's an old
White Russian fanatic named Aleksei Portenov. I know

who he is, and I know where to find him. What I want to know is, why!"

"A grudge against Josef Stalin?" Claire suggested.

Logan glanced at her. "Oh, come on, Hemmings. So far they've gone after FDR, and tried to erase the Versailles treaty. They're not out to settle some old score. They're trying to change the entire pattern of the twentieth century, and Stalin's just a handy handle. What Grigor said doesn't make sense! So I'm looking for something that does. Now show me the timebase you found."

From the mall maintenance sector they followed a rat path of piping tunnels, air ducts, and conduit shafts. At each twist and turn, Logan realized how thoroughly Hemmings must have researched this mission before launching. She never faltered, taking turn after turn, consulting her palm-scan only now and then. At a shaft intersection where their path was barred by a wide, vertical shaft with no catwalks or grid, she produced a miniaturized cable winch. She connected the little flair lock to a piping mount and cast the grapple across with one expert throw. It caught on a conduit sheath, and she winched the cable taut.

They crossed the shaft hand over hand, dangling above precipitous depths below. From the far side, Claire loosed the cable, snapped the flair free, and hauled in the entire rig. It made a package half the size of her small fist.

And Logan realized how she had managed to be so thoroughly prepared. "You used the sublimator, didn't you," he said. "ChronComp found the building plans for this place, and you speed-briefed on them."

"Of course." She nodded. "Not all of us cling to the Dark Ages, Logan. Technology is for using, not protesting."

Finally they reached the end of a large duct and peered through gridwork at a wide, brightly lit corridor all in white. Floors, ceilings, frames, and fixtures were pristine white, as were the coveralls of the guards patrolling there. The only colors visible were the heads, hands, and boot soles of the guards and the dark sheen of the guns they carried. Three were visible—two of them walking casual patrol past the vent, their footsteps fading into the distance to the right.

"This is a perimeter hallway," Claire whispered. "Like a horseshoe. They'll be gone about thirty minutes."

At the end of the corridor to the left, only a dozen yards from the grill where Logan and Hemmings hid, a gleaming white double door with a vivid black warning sign was guarded by a man with a businesslike submachine gun.

"Now what?" Logan inquired.

Claire shrugged. "I popped a steam vent to get in, the first time," she said. "They never knew they had company, just a leak. But I don't think that will work again."

"I wouldn't think so." Logan frowned. "Well, there's always the old-fashioned way."

Turning, he braced himself and kicked the grill outward. It clattered across the hall, its clatter echoed by a startled curse from the armed man at the door. Logan rolled to the side of the vent and crouched there, coiled and ready. It took the surprised guard only a moment to reach the open duct. He hesitated, hugged the wall, and stooped to peek inside. The hard fist that met him sent him tumbling clear across the hall.

Rubbing his outraged knuckles, Logan crawled out of the cramped air duct and stepped to the sprawled man. The guard was out cold. Stooping over him, Logan delivered a neck chop for good measure. It might be hours before the man regained consciousness. Logan dragged him across the hall and stuffed him into the air duct while Claire tidied up, sweeping bits of plaster and splintered wood into a little pile, which she tossed into the hole. She slung the submachine gun on her shoulder and went to the double door while Logan replaced the air vent. By the time he was done, she had the door open.

"If this place is legitimate," she said, "you owe a huge apology to at least one Canadian citizen."

"If this place is legitimate," he growled, "why doesn't TEC know all about it?"

He stepped through the door, looked around, and whistled. The room was a big, luxurious office, with glass walls overlooking a busy, arenalike area the size of a football stadium. Through tinted glass, they looked out across nests of cubicles, long rows of electronic equipment with monitor stations at intervals, and rising above it all, a building-sized monolithic enclosure that could be only one thing—the launch bays of a timesled.

"This is as far as I penetrated," Claire said. "Look over here."

Turning away from the glass wall, Logan grinned. The entire back wall of the office was a cluster of monitor screens rising above a single multiplex console.

"Command center," he muttered. "Whose office is this?"

"I don't know. There isn't a name or a clue. But whoever it is, is in charge. Everything is controlled from here." Claire indicated a system chart on one of the screens. "The whole complex is diagrammed. I don't think they have

E-warp. There's no Dome. But they sure have everything else that's needed for time-launch."

She reached toward the command console, and Logan said, "Wait. Can you scan for fingerprints?"

Claire glanced around. "The keyboard? Sure."

"Then scan it," he said. "Add the data to your TEC wafers. Note: print comparison to all retrieved items, missions AD840 and AD847."

"The Stella Raines encounters?" Claire's eyes narrowed. "You think this is her cubbyhole, Logan?"

"Call it a hunch," he said.

He watched critically while the blond agent's palm-scan recorded trace impressions on the keypads. Then he sat in front of the console and began typing.

"Now let's see if we can unscramble this thing," he mused.

Using a technique he had learned from Bob O'Donnelly in another life, he accessed the computer system diagnostics and tapped in a Maynard command code: locate and decode seven-digit randoms.

Giants are easy, O'Donnelly had quipped. The trick with giants is to find their weakness. Then you don't have to fight the whole giant, just one exposed nerve.

Am-Can's computer system was a giant—a linked megaframe whose hardware was similar to ChronComp's. But the giant wasn't ChronComp. It was only a computer.

At the speed of electron transfer, the big computer diagnosed itself, found those codes that Logan had persuaded it were viruses, and debugged itself.

Logan's delighted grin spread wide as the monitor banks came to life, free of security codes. Claire gasped her astonishment. "I didn't know that was possible!" she breathed.

"By God, it worked," Logan said. "Now let's see what this thing can tell us. What was the file code on that alternate eventuality program ChronComp scammed from Am-Can?"

Claire thought for a moment. "A word," she said. "It sounded Russian. Dos something."

"Dosvestia?" Logan keyed it in, and the center panel of screens went dark. But only for an instant. They lit again, in a dazzling display of historical interconnection. Time lines flowed and undulated, matched by rapidly scrolling sets of numbered data. Screen by screen, probability curves developed and intertwined. Then the scrolling stopped, and the screens synchronized. The year displayed was 2008. But the world described was not the world of now.

"It wasn't really Stalin at all," Claire breathed. "My God, Logan! Look what they're after!"

With disbelieving eyes, Logan looked at one display after another, letting them all come together in his mind. An alternate reality, analyzed and dissected—interlocking occurrences traced from event to subsequent event across a span of seven decades; the world as it would be today, given one slight change halfway around the world a long time ago. A world that still included the influences of Hitler and Tōjō, of Mussolini and Molotov and the rest of the conquerors, but without the ruthless counterbalance of Generalissimo Josef Stalin. Logan absorbed it and cursed, knowing the tracking was as flawless as any machine could make it.

"For want of a nail . . . ," he muttered.

What would the world now be, had Josef Stalin never achieved domination over the Eurasian Arc? It would be as portrayed here—a double empire spanning the Eastern Hemisphere, under the iron thumbs of the descendants of the ancient Teutons and boyars. The world of the White Russians of Byelorussia.

"That does it," Logan growled. "Do you have all this, Hemmings?"

"Better than that," she said. "With the codes debugged, we can direct-link ChronComp with this system. We'll have everything that's here."

"Then do it," Logan ordered. He stood, removed all the insignia from his uniform, and glanced once more at the scene beyond the glass—the spiderweb of a complete time complex with a launch device at its center. "You've got to get all this back to TEC, so make your link and use your retrieve."

She glanced around. "Aren't you coming?"

"I'm not out of time, remember? I got here in a packing crate. But you're twelve hours behind yourself, so get going!"

"Where are you going, Logan?"

"To find Aleksei Portenov," he said. "I want a closer look at Am-Can's time apparatus, then I'm going after the old man."

"Logan . . ."

He hesitated, and Claire came around the big console to stand before him, looking up into his eyes. Her expression was unreadable, but he found he couldn't break the eye contact . . . or didn't want to.

"Logan, in that other past of yours—the lost history— were we friends?"

He hesitated, then nodded. "Something like that, I guess. We didn't always get along, but there were times . . ."

"I thought so," she murmured. "The way you look at me, sometimes."

"Yeah. I called you Taffy, but not in public. You never liked nicknames."

Her eyes narrowed slightly. "Taffy? Why Taffy?"

"It's a contrary candy." He grinned. "Tough, stubborn stuff. Hard to chew and hard to swallow, but it is sweet to the tongue."

"Don't do anything dumb, Logan," she said softly. "I'm sort of getting used to you. I'd hate it if—"

"Don't say it." He smiled. "I can read your mind."

"Then what am I thinking?"

"You're thinking about my lost past, and how it might feel to be cancelled out, like me. And you're thinking there's a timesled down there that could take me back to 1930 if I wanted it to, and that I might not be able to resist a chance to undo the changes that make this your world but not mine. And I suppose you're wondering just how far my oath as a time enforcement officer can be trusted, in view of—"

"Logan." She hadn't moved, but it seemed her eyes were closer now—as though the world around them was shrinking, down and down until there wasn't really anything else to see but those deep-sea eyes, gazing up at him from the shadow of her honey-blond hair.

"What, Hemmings?"

"You're a fraud, Logan. You aren't reading my mind. I'm not thinking any such thing."

"What, then?"

"I'm thinking," she said, "what a shame it would be if

I—the me of this time, of right now—were to never see you again. Take care of yourself, Logan. Do what's right, and take care of yourself."

For a long moment they stood like that, sharing words that were not spoken. Then he turned away, abruptly. "See you around, Hemmings."

"When?"

"Some time," he said.

TEC Headquarters

It was a stunned and solemn group that gathered around the monitors in TEC's briefing room. They had just witnessed the cold reality of an alternate present world, displayed for them by ChronComp from its search of the Am-Can data banks.

It was real—as real as the progressive logic of giant computers could make it—and it was harsh. It was the utopia of Dosvestia.

On their screens, they had seen a world enslaved—like something right out of the Dark Ages. A world in which technology had progressed only marginally since the great wars that divided the Eastern Hemisphere into two superpowers—the Axis Alliance that ruled all of Europe and controlled a great arc of geography from the Mediterranean Sea to the South China Sea, and the Russo-Cathayan Empire that sat astride Asia from the Balkans to Japan.

The rest of the world—the Americas, Australia, and the South Pacific—was a rough hegemony of secondary states held in joint fief by the great powers. It was a world in which 98 percent of the population was in the service of, or in bondage to, a handful of absolute rulers.

Peasant farmers plowed the rich lowlands along the Mississippi with oxen in harness, while sleek rocket-jet ships of the privileged scouted the skies above. The once-great cities were decimated, serving now only as counting houses for the squalid resources of dominated lands.

The vision went on and on, in horrifying detail. This was what the present could be, if a few fanatics with time travel fulfilled their dreams.

The alternate reality was simple in its origin. A single linchpin was removed from the established history of the world, and everything from there forward toppled like dominoes.

"His name was Joseph," Dr. Dale Easter recited. "Or Josef, in direct translation from the Cyrillic. Josef Vissarionovich Dzhugashvili. He was born in Gori, in the Transcaucasian region of Georgia, in 1879—the son of a poor shoemaker and a deeply religious washerwoman. His schooling was a theological seminary at Tbilisi. It was there he came under the influence of Marxist doctrine, probably through the writings of V. I. Lenin.

"As a youth, Josef was an agitator and a propagandist, and at the turn of the century he was expelled from seminary for disloyal views. He was deported to Siberia, but escaped from there and joined the Bolsheviks. He participated in the revolutions of 1905, 1912, and finally in the March Revolution in 1917. Hardly anyone at the time paid note to Josef Dzhugashvili. He was just a little man, overshadowed by the likes of Lenin, Trotsky, Zinovyev, and the others, but through all those years he worked ruthlessly from within, to gain control of the revolution for himself.

"Josef was rarely noticed in the early seasons of the Bolshevik era in Russia, but he was always there, and by 1922 he made himself secretary-general of the Communist Party. It was some time after that that he adopted a new name, a Russian name—Stalin. It means *man of steel*."

"One man," Eugene Matuzek muttered, staring at the screens where a drab, hopeless 2008 continued to unfold in painful detail. "One little man, and he made this much difference."

"An evil little man," Easter corrected. "And an opportunist. It was an age of rampaging egos, and Stalin fit right in. Hitler, Roosevelt, General Tōjō, Mussolini, Franco, Churchill—they all came together in the 1930s and '40s to play out a little game called domination, with the world as their gaming board. And there was Stalin, right in the middle of it, playing all the sides against one another and picking up the pieces. He came to epitomize the great fiction of Communism. It's taken three generations to even begin to heal the scars of that game called World War II, but the healing was possible because there was always a balance of power, even among the evils.

"What we're seeing here—what that quiet little menace called Dosvestia has always seen—is another kind of outcome. Please notice who controls Eurasia in this alternate reality. The predominant dynasty is the family Portenov. Aleksei would have been born a prince, if it hadn't been for that little monster Josef Stalin."

Amy Fuller seemed pale and frightened as she considered the significance of what Claire Hemmings had brought back from Toronto. "But—but if Portenov were to change history this much, his would change, too. He'd never know what he had done."

"He doesn't care," Claire said. "He's a fanatic. He doesn't give a damn what the consequences are—for anybody—so long as he gets his way."

At the farthest corner of the table, Charles Graham nodded. "It seems that way," he said. "The man is obviously insane, but so have some of our greatest leaders been, all down through history. The common characteristic seems to be, 'take it or break it, I want it, it's mine.'"

"You'll notice in my scans that Am-Can doesn't have E-warp capability," Claire agreed. "There's no Dome, nothing to show what the effects of any time alteration might be until they show up as accomplished history. A timesled, but no E-warp. That's like having atomic capability without social conscience. They simply don't care."

"Well, we have E-warp," Matuzek growled. "And I'd say we had better eat, sleep, and breathe ripples until we get to the bottom of this." He turned to Hemmings. "Where did you say Logan went?"

"He said he was going after Portenov," Claire told him.

"And you couldn't stop him, or at least go with him?"

"I was out of time, Captain. I was in the last hour of a twelve-hour retrosync. I was just about to be in two places at the same time, with a computer linkup that had to be completed at this end before this evidence could be delivered. Logan went on his own time, without TEC insignia or credentials. He completed our mission as ordered, then went on, acting on his own."

"You might have stopped him, Hemmings."

"Maybe." She shrugged. "I'm not sure Jack Logan can be stopped when he makes up his mind."

"Sorry." Matuzek nodded. "Of course, you did what you had to do."

"So Jack Logan is still out there, somewhere," Easter mused. "A walking paradox without credentials, operating at his own volition and on his own time. And now he has access to a time-travel facility that isn't ours?"

"He has credentials," Graham noted. "U.S. Secret Service, special detail. I arranged it myself."

"Yes, sir." Easter nodded. "But we don't really know this guy, do we? We've accepted him as a paradoxer, and ChronComp has his evaluations. But he has no past! He exists in our reality only because he was out of the continuum when our reality separated from his."

"He has no more idea why that happened than our research people do," Matuzek pointed out. "But we're working on it. We've been over every detail of the 1930 mission a dozen times. We'll find it if we have to sift through those events a second at a time."

The historian nodded. "I know we'll find out why," he said. "My concern is what. We have theories about parallel time lines, but we really don't know what happens to one history when another history veers off from it. Does it just go on, separately, or does it disappear? Is Logan's time line still out there somewhere, with his past in it? Or is there only one time line?" He removed his glasses and squinted at Matuzek, across the table. "It's deep stuff, Captain. Nobody knows the answers."

Eugene Matuzek took a deep breath. "Like what happens when an accomplished anachronism is reversed? Let's stop dancing around this thing, people. If Jack Logan's gone renegade, there's no telling what might happen. He'd be a loose cannon, with access to the past!"

"Logan's no loose cannon!" Claire cut in. "I'd stake my life on that."

"You are, Hemmings." Easter spread his hands. "We're all staking our lives on it."

X

Toronto, Ontario
2008

Logan closed the white doors behind him and checked the time. It would be close, for Claire Hemmings. She had a computer linkup to achieve, accesses and routes to find, and codes to implant so that the Am-Can megaframe would introduce itself to ChronComp out there in the network and spill its guts. He paused for a moment at the replaced air vent, heard the steady breathing of the unconscious man behind it, then sprinted along the curving hallway until he found what he was looking for—a side alcove leading to a pair of washrooms.

It was less than a minute later when the two roving guards appeared again on their rounds, strolling casually toward the command center. They passed the toilet alcove, and Logan took them from behind. They never knew what hit them.

"I've bought you a little time, Taffy," he muttered wryly. "Use it well."

Minutes later, garbed in the white pullover of one of the guards, Jack Logan slipped through the perimeter security of the Dosvestia timebase, deep within Am-Can's secret Toronto complex, and headed for the sled bays.

The best camouflage in any penetration is to avoid attention, and the best way to avoid attention in a workplace is to seem to belong there. White-suited technicians barely glanced at him as he strolled through the installation, his eyes missing nothing. Here and there were guard stations, but they were easily avoided. Only when he approached the control room of the timefield itself was there tight security, but he didn't have to actually enter the area to see what he wanted to see. Through glass observation panels he studied the vectoring controls, the tachyon ignition fail-safes, and the launch ramps beyond.

As Claire had said, the entire system was virtually a carbon copy of TEC's timesled controls, and it took only a moment for the timecop to locate and memorize the auto-launch overrides. TEC had such overrides built into its system—an emergency launch capability in the event of invasion or catastrophic breakdown. The overrides had never been activated, so far as Logan knew, but they were there just in case.

And as a duplicate of TEC's system, Am-Can's had them, too.

When he had satisfied his curiosity, Logan retraced his steps to the main entrance. But this time he didn't bother to circumvent the sensors. This time, going out, he simply walked through the scans, feeling the cameras on him as they reacted to his passage. Somewhere in the distance an alarm sounded, then another and another, but by then Jack Logan was past the gate and gone, down the long hallway that led to a bank of elevators. He selected one, rode the lift to the fourteenth floor of the Eaton Grand, and stepped out into a crowded, busy foyer with plate windows all along one wall.

The man who stepped out of the elevator there, and into the next lift down, was a tired, slump-shouldered, off-duty security officer in a white coverall with Am-Can insignia. The man who left that elevator at the first level of Eaton Center was a tall, trim man whose slightly military attire was almost as dark as his thick hair and bore no insignia at all.

At a mall restaurant he stopped for a steak sandwich—real, nonsoy beef like the U.S. should have had, but for this history's bizarre trade relations between neighboring countries—then he disappeared into the crowds thronging the great mall's corridors. A busy commuter shuttle at the north entrance sported bright signs displaying routes and schedules, which Logan studied. He keyed NSA's field fund number into a service vendor and arranged for a car. A number, description, and magnetic key appeared at the slot, and he pocketed them. Again checking the time, he boarded the eastbound shuttle to Newcastle. The rented car would be waiting for him there, and he would double back to Oshawa. He already had the location, address, and description of the place he was going, along with a security procedure analysis that he had obtained from Am-Can's obliging computer.

Nearly two hours had passed now, since he tripped the alarms at Am-Can's timebase. "You know by now that I'm coming for you, Aleksei," he muttered to himself. "You've had plenty of time to sweat, swear, and switch to a backup plan for time alteration. You want to change the world, Aleksei? Well, this is your last chance, because I'll be there in forty-five minutes."

Logan hoped the Dome at TEC headquarters was being monitored closely. He suspected there was about to be one hell of a ripple.

Oshawa, Ontario

When the alarms were tripped at Am-Can in Toronto, the alert went directly to the secluded estate of Aleksei Portenov in Oshawa. Within minutes, the monitors in the gold room were spelling out a scenario of disaster, while the old man huddled beneath his comforter and muttered curses in three languages.

Logan! The man known as Jack Logan. He had been delivered to the sealed warehouse adjoining Eaton Center, but then—somehow—he had escaped. Now Grigor was dead, the doctor was dead, and all the careful schemes and meticulous plans fostered by Dosvestia lay in ruins.

The man had gone everywhere, seen everything! He had walked through the timelabs as casually as a tourist. He had seen the launch-control bays. He had even tapped into Am-Can's megaframes and somehow deleted all the safeguards there. He had—and the computer faithfully registered the access—reviewed the alternate history that was Dosvestia's goal. Then, as though throwing down a gauntlet, he had intentionally tripped the security systems and posed before the scanning cameras!

Who was this Logan, that he could do all this?

At the old man's order, Vassili set up a multinational conference via dedicated satellite, and Aleksei looked from one to another of the faces staring back at him on banked monitors. Dosvestia, he thought. *All that remains* of the grand scheme, after all these years—pale, timeworn faces devoid of the thrill of revolution. Aleksei scowled. These are old men! he told himself. These are not White Russia anxious to reclaim its powers and its privileges, these are just old dodderers. They have lost heart. They will panic and falter in the face of disaster.

On the verge of reporting the penetration of Am-Can security, Aleksei changed his mind. Now was not the time for committees. Now was the time for decisive action.

"The hour is at hand, comrades," he told them now. "The little games are over, and it is time to strike. Say whatever good-byes you will, it does not matter. A new history is about to emerge, and it will be the only reality. Your children and grandchildren will rule half a world, and it will always have been so. *Dosvedanya*, old comrades. We will not know one another again . . . not in this life."

At his signal, Vassili touched a button, and the gaping faces on the banked monitors winked out.

Triggering the hand-rest controls on his chair, Aleksei Portenov turned and—for the first time in many years—looked directly at his retainer. "You will go, this time, Vassili. There have been enough failures. Stella Ilyanova is not available now. She is still back in 1971, on the mission I gave her. But it doesn't matter. It is time for the coup de grâce."

Vassili shuffled his feet, looking uneasy. Aleksei thumbed a key and tapped a handpad, and the big screen above his desk came alive—a picture of a man in old-fashioned military dress. The man was obviously small in stature, sturdy and compact, but there was power in the steady gaze of those narrowed, brooding eyes and in the stubborn set of a square chin beneath a heavy mustache.

"Stalin." Aleksei nodded. "Josef Vissarionovich Stalin. Do you remember Transylvania, Vassili, when you were younger? All those men you killed at Tbilisi, do you remember how you killed them?"

Lowering his big, shaggy head, Vassili nodded.

"You will kill this man the way you killed those, Vassili. Listen carefully, now. You will go immediately to Toronto, to the timesled. It will be waiting for you. It will place you in the month of March, the year 1917, in Moscow. Stalin will not look like this, Vassili. He will be much younger, but you will know him. You will find him in the office of *Pravda*, and there you will kill him."

Vassili gazed at his master with pleading eyes, and Aleksei flicked a reassuring hand. "It will be all right, Vassili. I know that I will not be here when you return, but you will have your reward." He gestured around them, at the priceless treasures of the gold room. "All this will be yours, Vassili. Just kill Stalin in 1917, and when you return, you may claim everything here as your own. Now go, Vassili, quickly! *Dosvedanya*, faithful servant. Go!"

Aleksei did not see Vassili again, though he heard the big man striding along the outer halls, preparing himself for his mission. And, of course, footfalls were all he heard. Vassili had been a peaceful Croatian farmer once, more than a decade ago. But Serb rebels had come, and Vassili carried the scars of their visit. They had cut out his tongue. In the years following, many a Serbian sympathizer had regretted that the rebels left Vassili alive.

Aleksei busied himself at his computer, feeding vector codes and mission data into the megaframe at Am-Can, preparing the timesled there for Vassili's arrival. After a while, he heard the helicopter take off from the estate roof, and he leaned back, tired and sated.

"Vassili, you idiot," he muttered wryly. "What other man would go on such a mission and not realize that once history is changed, he can never return because time travel will not have been discovered?"

An alarm sounded, distantly, and Aleksei Portenov knew what it was. When he heard the bell that signaled the breech of the main gate, he was certain. Like the Nemesis of myth, like implacable destiny, the man called Logan had arrived.

TEC Headquarters
3:15 A.M.

The ripple on the Dome was monstrous—a level-six anachronism centered at March 28, 1917, its location a section of old buildings just south of the Kremlin in the city of Moscow.

"*Pravda!*" Dale Easter announced, trailing maps and satellite navigation charts behind him as he hurried into the briefing room. "We've got a fix on location. It's the printing plant where *Pravda* was published at the start of the Bolshevik Revolution. Josef Stalin had just returned from Siberia, that March, and taken over his old job as editor."

"Then this is Dosvestia again," Matuzek said. "They're still after Stalin."

He glanced at the day board and frowned. Line after line of the timecop roster carried "Off Duty" flags. Malone and Spinetti were on assignment—back to 1984 to stop a home-project jumper from altering a will—and the two male backups, Reeves and Jefferson, had launched in response to a minor blip centered on the Oklahoma City Federal Building, 1995.

"Damned tourists!" the captain growled. "Okay, who's up?"

"Just me." Julie Price stepped forward. "Four other agents are on their way in, but it'll be at least twenty minutes."

Matuzek gazed thoughtfully at the girl. Though a fully qualified timecop and field agent, Julie still had the fresh, unspoiled appearance of a high school cheerleader. Her auburn hair was a bouncing ponytail and the severe, gray field uniform she wore did no more than emphasize her slight, agile form. As always, Eugene Matuzek had to curb his fatherly instincts to even consider sending Julie on a time mission. He always felt as though he were throwing a favorite niece to the wolves.

But there was no alternative now, short of making this launch himself, and with Jack Logan out running loose somewhere, the captain had to be in his office.

"All right," he growled. "Julie, you're it. Suit up. The clock's running and this is a big one."

"I'll go with her," Claire Hemmings blurted, bursting through the open door. "This is a team-of-two launch, Captain. O'Donnelly can handle the sublimator for us. I'll suit up."

"The hell you will," Matuzek snapped. "You're the only systems analyst I have. I can't have you out on assignment when Logan turns up. You might be the only one he'll listen to, if he's gone renegade."

"Well, Julie can't go by herself!" Claire snapped. "You know damned well this is a team job, whatever it is!"

There were scuffling sounds at the door, and Bob O'Donnelly scurried in, busily strapping on the flak cloth and webbing of a launch suit. "No sweat," he said. "I'll be ready to launch in five minutes."

Dale Easter gaped at the young ThinkTanker. "You're a historian!" he rasped.

"Of course I am." O'Donnelly grinned. "But I'm current in field technique. I requalified six months ago. Timelaw, warrant process, launch simulation, arrest and intervention procedures—the whole bit. Also, I speak a little Russian." He turned his determined grin on Matuzek. "If you have another choice, call it, Captain. Otherwise, clear me and let's get on with this."

Matuzek sighed and shook his head, slowly. "All right. God help us, you two are it," he said.

"A cybernetics whiz kid and a teenybopper," Easter muttered, looking pale. "And a level-six ripple on max warp. God help us all."

"Don't sweat it, old-timer," O'Donnelly purred. "A lot of actual, real-live people were young once, you know. By the way, I forget—which end of a nine-millimeter handgun are you supposed to point, to propel a projectile in the direction you intend it to go?"

"That's not funny, O'Donnelly!" Matuzek rumbled. "Easter, give ChronComp its head on this one. Reference Stalin, 1917 Moscow, and the Bolshevik Revolution, and feed all the specifics you can into the speed-brief. Hemmings, you handle the sublimator. Let's go, people! Launch in eight! Whatever caused that ripple has already happened, and it's coming down now! We'll set insertion for thirty minutes prior." Matuzek headed for the launch bay, herding his team along with him. As Bob O'Donnelly brushed past him, the captain snapped, "You point the end with the hole in it, you damned smart aleck."

Moscow
1917

A simulation is to a time-launch as a playful kitten is to a hungry tiger. Bob O'Donnelly had heard that comparison somewhere, but until the moment he strapped into the second seat of the timesled, he had no idea how accurate it was.

"Just relax," Julie's voice murmured in his ear as he placed his headset and tightened his cinches. "Remember, a timesled might kill you, but it won't hurt you. Pain doesn't register at tach speeds."

"That's a comforting thought," he assured the unseen girl three feet away in the forward compartment. "Thank you."

"Just remember," she added, "trust your trusses. Don't try to brace yourself against the G-forces. You'll only break your neck or something, if you do. And I've found it helps to concentrate on something silly—like an old song or something."

"Okay," he breathed as the voice of doom began its serene, cheerful countdown. "'Twas brillig, and the slithy toves did gyre and gimble in the wabe . . .'"

"Thrust programmed," the mechanical voice droned. "Tachyon drive ignition in five . . . four . . . three . . ."

"'All mimsy were the borogoves,'" O'Donnelly whispered, beginning to sweat. "'And the mome raths out—'"

" . . . two . . . one . . . contact. "

The tachyon thrusters pounded into awful life, and the sled hurtled from the bay, down the far-too-short track with the ominous wall ahead. Stained by past failures, the wall loomed just beyond the great armatures that generated three of the four components of a time-space wormhole. The sled itself, providing it attained the critical Q-velocity of 2,994 fps, would be the fourth part of the equation.

For an awful instant Bob O'Donnelly found himself crushed backward against steel-hard padding, while track markers shot past too quickly to count and the massive, stain-marked wall loomed just ahead. Then sudden lightnings flashed and thundered as the timefield sprang to life, and sled, passengers, and reality all collapsed into a nothingness beyond description . . . and out again, in a reality that was nothing like the world just vacated.

Upside down, in free fall, O'Donnelly tumbled a few feet through icy air and crashed down onto the bow-suspended top of a closed carriage. Bows sang and snapped, fabric ripped away, and the historian thumped down onto the floorboards of the vehicle. He lit on his shoulders, his legs flailing, and looked up into the startled, fur-shrouded faces of four passengers—two bearded men and two shawl-bundled women.

He stared at them, they stared at him, then one of the men shouted an angry challenge and half drew a gleaming saber from within the folds of his heavy fur coat. In the crowded carriage, his arm was blocked and the draw was not completed, but his sentiments were clear.

O'Donnelly scuttled backward, found a latch, and yanked it.

"'Beware the Jabberwock!'" he squeaked.

The carriage door behind him popped open and he half jumped, half fell outward to fall facedown into six inches of fresh snow marred by the tracks of horses and wagons.

The crunching hooves of a draft team narrowly missed him as he rolled frantically, dodged by iron-rimmed wheels, and scurried to the narrow footpath running alongside the thoroughfare. Hordes of shabby, thick-coated people mingled there. Some among them carried baskets on poles or pushed barrows laden with muddy tubers, loaves of bread, and icy, slithering fish. Not far away rang the cries of vendors in a street market. From the shadows of a littered, drifted alley, O'Donnelly peered this way and that, and finally caught sight of his partner. Julie was perched on a ledge ten feet up the side of a smoke-darkened building, scanning the crowds below.

She was attracting more attention than Bob was. People passing him tended to glance his way curiously, then go about their business. But all along the street, surprised gazes turned toward the girl on the ledge. It was more than just her location that held their attention, he deduced. Slim and lithe, clad in her tight, formfitting launch suit, Julie fit in with the Moscow street crowd like a mink among bears.

He waved and shouted to get her attention, then pushed through a crowd of vendors to meet her as she swung down from the ledge and dropped to the street.

"Let's get out of this crowd before somebody gets rough," he suggested.

A block away on a side street, they found the printing plant that produced the Moscow edition of *Pravda*. The newspaper had only recently moved its operation from St. Petersburg, and its quarters were abominable, but the place was full of busy, deadly serious people turning out propaganda for the next phase of Lenin's revolution. Armed men met them inside the door, barking questions and eyeing the odd-looking weapons at their hips. But O'Donnelly bluffed them down, and the two timecops slipped past.

In a shedlike closet in the back of the building they found piles of collected clothing and helped themselves, hiding their uniforms under shabby woolen long coats, dirty hats, and shawls.

Then they eased into the printing plant and tried to make themselves invisible while they waited. They had already spotted the little man with the big mustache. At thirty-eight years of age, Josef Stalin was in his early prime. And with the Bolshevik Revolution under way, he was in his element. Traces of iron gray already marked his thick, close-cropped hair, and the twenty years of arrests, imprisonments, deportations, and escapes gave his square, serious face the look of an older man.

"He looks like Brian Donlevy with a mustache," Julie whispered, as they watched the editor of *Pravda* directing the feverish activities around him.

O'Donnelly glanced at her. "Who?"

"An old movie star, from back in the forties or fifties. Brian Donlevy. Stalin looks a little like him."

"Oh." O'Donnelly shrugged, then pointed. "Well, there's one that looks like Bela Lugosi, only bigger."

Beyond the clattering row of presses in the main room was an open door leading to an alleyway where a flatbed wagon was being unloaded. The big man who had appeared there seemed to fill the doorway as he hesitated, squinting, looking around. He towered over the busy Russians around him, as a great, shaggy bear over lesser bears. A fur hat sat aslant on his big, ugly head, and he was draped from neck to knees in a heavy cloak that could double as a blanket.

"Somebody lose a nightmare?" O'Donnelly whispered.

Beside him, crouched in the shadows of a pile of crates of paper, Julie's hand went to the gun at her waist. "Yeah," she said. "Well, that nightmare is wearing 1990s snow boots. Look sharp, O'Donnelly. He's our ripple!"

As she said it, the blanket cloak in the doorway shifted and parted, and beneath it they glimpsed a huge fist holding a sawed-off, double-barreled shotgun of the period.

"It's an assassination," Julie hissed. "He's after Stalin."

O'Donnelly clenched her shoulder and pointed. "Stalin's over there, beyond those stacked crates. Keep him out of sight. I'll be right back."

Before she could protest, the historian was gone, hurrying across the printing room. At the fourth press he knelt, busying himself with something on the floor while a trio of bearded revolutionaries passed, and when he stood again he was holding a length of slack rope. He intercepted a group of workmen carrying bales of paper, barked a command in Russian, and headed for the open door. Obediently, the porters fell in behind him. O'Donnelly approached "Bela Lugosi," glanced up at him, then muttered something in Russian and pushed past, forcing the big man to edge backward, out of the doorway. O'Donnelly stepped out into the gray, snowbound alley, and the porters followed him, all lugging heavy bales on their shoulders.

Julie took advantage of the moment to slip across the

printing room, to the stacks. Josef Stalin was there, reviewing sheafs of handwritten prose by the light of an oil lamp while several younger men stood around him, waiting.

Keep him out of sight, O'Donnelly had said. Damn you, Bob, Julie thought, I'm supposed to be senior agent here. What are you doing?

At the copy table, Stalin handed papers to one of the young men and gestured toward the north corner, where typesetters worked their galleys. The younger man bowed slightly, turned, and his hand brushed an inkwell, spilling its contents onto the littered floor. He started to apologize, but Stalin waved him away. He hurried past Julie, on his way to the composition tables.

And Julie saw her opportunity. Grabbing an inkpot from a nearby shelf, she opened it and stepped around the crates, stooping to retrieve the fallen inkwell. The men gathered around Stalin only glanced at her, then ignored her. Covered by a tattered greatcoat, her hair scarf-wrapped and hidden under an old hat, she was only a serf-class girl come to clean up the mess.

From the great room, she heard shouting voices and the sounds of things falling. "O'Donnelly," she whispered. She stood, set the inkwell on the table near Josef Stalin, and stepped around closer to him as the other men turned away, curious at the noise from the print shop.

Stalin looked up from his work. "Who are you?" he demanded in Russian. As he started to stand, Julie bumped him with her elbow, then quickly and methodically poured ink all over him.

The future dictator of the Union of Soviet Socialist Republics gasped, cursed, and wiped black hands across his face. Julie shrieked convincingly, backed away, and scuttled into the cover of a stack of wooden pallets. The men around Stalin gaped at him, then brought out cloths and soiled print rags to wipe him down.

He cursed in at least two Slavic languages, waved them away, and headed for the little wash shed at the back of the alcove.

"I guess that should do it," Julie muttered. Slipping through the stacks, she went to see how her partner was getting along with Bela Lugosi.

She found O'Donnelly out in the slush-deep alley, applying a come-along to the wrists of the big time jumper. People had gathered around to gawk, but they kept their distance, even backing away as O'Donnelly raised the big, sawed-off shotgun over his head to wave at Julie.

"One jabberwock, ready for delivery." The historian grinned as Julie came through the crowd. "This gentleman's not talking. He's from our time, though, and I have his retrieval unit in my pocket. It's another of those Am-Can jobs. The techs might learn something from it, don't you think?"

"You're darn right, they can." Julie grinned. "They can get its retrieval coordinates. How did you do this, Bob?"

"Simple." He shrugged. "I tied a rope to one of the presses inside, then came out here and tied the other end to a dray wagon. When I slapped the wheelhorse, the team bolted, and out came the press, and it brought this big guy here with it. He may have a broken leg, but I think he's just bruised up a little. How's Stalin?"

"Stained," Julie said. With a last quick look around at the bleak, depressing ugliness of revolutionary Russia, she took her hold on O'Donnelly's come-along and touched her wrist retrieve.

O'Donnelly was almost preening himself, standing over the bound prisoner. "I did pretty well, for a first mission, didn't I!"

Julie's smile was a ray of sunshine. "We both did okay, I guess," she agreed. "For a whiz kid and a teenybopper."

The odd disappearance of three strangers from an alley behind the Iskra Dasi printing shop—in broad daylight and before dozens of witnesses—would be talked about for a while in Moscow, but it was never mentioned in *Pravda* or in any other periodical. The heroes of the Bolshevik Social Revolution were far too stern and serious a group to concern themselves with vodka-induced hallucinations.

Denver, Colorado
1971

They drove out to Denver after the first snow, to hear a performance of some of Harry's music at the Antlers Theater. In all the years he had been composing for others, it was the first time a major presentation of his themes had been performed in concert, and Harry was invited as one of the guests of honor.

It was a long drive—out across the bleak, rising high plains to the snowy Rockies—but it gave them an opportunity to visit Jimmy and Tammy in their new location. Kaki made up her mind that they were going, and—as always—Harry agreed.

"Whatever pleases you, hon," he drawled, "just tickles me half to death."

And so it was that on a bitter-crisp day, on a mountainside north of Denver, Jimmy Sheffield gave his parents a personal tour of the camp at Paxton Peak and the mysteries hidden within a quartz-crystal cavern.

"It's really amazing," he said, as they prowled through narrow, brightly lit offshoots of the main cave. "So far, we've come up with at least three new theories of dimensional resonance that nobody has been able to shoot down."

"Dimensional resonance." Harry nodded. "I remember thinking of music that way, when I was a kid. Maybe I always have."

"Yeah." Jimmy grinned at his father. "I know. That's where I got the idea, from you. I remember you saying that music has more dimensions than any other art form. I guess I got hooked on that analogy. My part of this . . . this 'magic' we're doing here is to define it as we go, and I tend to think in terms of resonance: harmonics, tonal sequence—all the concepts you taught me."

"And you're developing a new science from it?"

"Maybe it will be, someday. We're doing some things that haven't been done before." He gestured toward the main chamber, where people attended banks of sophisticated instruments in the midst of mind-numbing webworks of fine electronic wire—a vast nest of filaments connecting sensory instruments to the various forms and facets of the living crystal. "Let me show you something," he said.

Mac Wainwright and Charlie Wang were in the cave, along with several technicians and graduate students who had joined the eventuality-wave program in the past month. The little campsite on the mountainside had become a village of trailers, campers, and even a couple of slap-up cabins. Jimmy looked over Mac Wainwright's shoulder for a moment, then asked, "Mac, can you pull up your sensor patterns on the main screen, for my folks?"

"Sure thing." Mac nodded. He keyed in an access code, tapped selections into a computer menu, and the screen displayed a flowing, undulating pattern of graphics, annotated with numeric formulae.

"What does that remind you of?" Jimmy pointed.

"A visual symphony," Harry Sheffield said.

"Time," Kaki said.

Jimmy and Mac both turned to her. "Time?"

"It looks like a time track." She shrugged. "What is it?"

Jimmy and Mac glanced at each other while Charlie Wang got out a spiral pad and scrawled some notes into it.

"It's what our sensors pick up from the crystalline structure here," Mac explained. "But we don't know what it is. That's what our study is all about."

"We've viewed it as a musical pattern," Jimmy said. "The same as you, Dad. The mathematics of it track harmonic math, and when I applied your dimensional harmonics ideas to it, they seemed to fit—peaks and valleys representing Dimension One, the scrolling effect D-Two, the loops and contours D-Three. But that's where it loses us. It acts as though it's trying to illustrate a further dimension, but there isn't another dimension."

"Yes, there is," Kaki observed. "It's time."

Harry was studying the patterns on the screen. "I could almost play this," he muttered. "Your mother's right, Jimmy. There are four dimensions to music. Harmonics don't have physical limits. There's pitch, volume, and resonance, but there's also duration. Tenure is a basic element of harmonics. And that means time."

"Time," Charlie Wang said, as though to himself. "Of course there's time. We hadn't considered that, in our equations. Mac, can you run a—"

"I'm already doing it," Mac said, looking up from his

keyboard. "I think it works. Watch the screen, when I give the pattern a fourth vector."

The undulating flow on the screen seemed to come to life, exploding outward to fill the screen with infinitely complex subpatterns.

"I want to see this in hologram," Charlie breathed. "If a two-dimensional screen will approximate three dimensions, I wonder what a three-dimensional screen will do."

"And whether it'll show us the rest of the resonance," Mac added.

"It will if you know how to look at it," Kaki said positively. "I told you, harmonic analogies aside, what you have here is a picture of time."

They stayed overnight with Jimmy, Tammy, and the kids, and visited the cave laboratory one more time the following morning, before heading home.

"I've got to tell you, Mrs. Sheffield," Mac told Kaki. "You have either set us back three months or opened a whole new avenue for us. Most of us worked all night on the time premise, and so far we can't find a flaw in it. If it proves out, then we'll know what these new sensors are attuned to. Time! Though Heaven only knows what we'll do with time harmonics, if that's what we're tracking."

"You'll think of something." Kaki smiled. "There'll be a use for E-warp, once you invent it."

"You think we're going to invent eventuality-wave resonance technology?"

"Of course you are," she assured him. "Somebody has to."

When the elder Sheffields were safely away, on their return trip to Nebraska, Mac Wainwright got Jimmy

Sheffield aside. "Your mother's weird," he said. "Is she always like that?"

"I've only known her all my life," Jimmy admitted. "But, usually, yes. I've always wondered, secretly, if my mother really came from this planet."

Coming into the outskirts of Boulder, Harry Sheffield glanced quizzically at his wife. "You practically told them," he said. "About temporal theory, time travel . . . you virtually handed E-warp to them on a platter. Aren't you afraid of anachronism anymore?"

Kaki's graying hair and the little traces of time in her face did nothing at all to detract from the smile she gave him. "I thought it was about time," she said. "Somebody has to invent E-warp before Kleindast ever begins to develop time travel. He had eventuality patterns to work with. It might as well be our son and his friends who do that."

"I guess you're right." Harry nodded. "What changed your mind, though? Why this sudden unveiling of your mysterious past?"

The smile left her face, and her eyes grew serious. "Do you remember me telling you that the people across the street have a tenant for their garage apartment? Well, I saw her—the new tenant—just before we left home. It was the first time I had really noticed her. Harry, I knew that woman! I remember her from a long time ago, from the future, and she hasn't changed at all. Her name is Stella Raines, and she was one of my instructors at TEC Academy. She's from the future, Harry! And she's living right across the street from our house!"

"Everything that I am now, I owe to an old trove of gold coins." Aleksei's thin, ancient voice had a hollow sound on the wafer playback. Logan leaned forward to turn up the volume, glancing wryly at the old man in the wheelchair.

"I was to board a train that day," the recorded voice continued. "It was the C3, to Detroit. It was part of a planned holiday to the Chicago World's Fair. But when those young people from the States arrived with their little treasure, I tarried. I was young then, and full of quick ambitions. Franklin Roosevelt had just become president in the States, and I was dabbling in American gold. So many people were trying to sell their gold before the new regime took it.

"But these old coins that the young couple brought! They were more than just metal. This was a treasure of historic significance. I have always felt that those coins were meant for me—like talismans. I missed my train that day, and it was on that day that the C3 derailed, killing thirty-nine people.

"The incident confirmed for me that my destiny was to live, to correct the inequities of history. It was after that that I located some of the old Dosvestia members and revitalized that great cause.

"Everything that followed was as implacable as destiny. I was not even surprised three years ago when a man in my employ—a United States senator—came to my people at Am-Can with plans for a time-travel device."

Logan thumbed the playback's pause and shook his head. For all its luxury, its gracious, elegant architecture, and the veiled ostentation of its fenced, kept grounds, the estate of Alex Porter was a cold, forbidding place. To Logan, it reeked of sick ambition, and the old man gazing up at him from a mechanized wheelchair was the source.

Getting in had been no real problem. There had been two guards at the gate, but when Logan flashed his U.S. Secret Service credentials, their resolve had evaporated. And when he suggested that the RCMP would require their presence for questioning, they had both become very scarce. The only other people he had encountered on his way into the house were a couple of hired servants, who likewise wanted nothing to do with the authorities.

Now, apparently, Logan and the old man had the place to themselves, and he was listening to the rambling memoirs that Aleksei Portenov was completing when the timecop came in.

"What did you mean to do with these recordings?" he asked the old man curiously. "Memoirs, maybe? If you'd changed history, as you planned, these would be gone right along with everything else. So what's the purpose?"

"Not gone," the old man said. "A printed copy of all but the conclusion has been deposited in a safe place. It will come to my attention—that other 'me' of the new time line—in the prime of my life. Then I will know that my world—my proper world, where I and my peers hold the power, as we should—did not just happen. I will know that in another life I took the necessary steps to restore my preferred history."

"You are insane, Aleksei Portenov," Logan mused, looking around at the vast wealth of the gold room. He had never seen so much precious metal all in one place—artifacts, jewelry, statuary, and coins, thousands of coins.

"And I suppose you have a plan for all this, too? Some way to take it with you into your alternate world?"

Aleksei sighed. "Toys." He shrugged, under his woolen shawl. "Simple pastimes, for my amusement while destiny took its course." The ancient eyes held Logan's curiously. "Why do you think that I'm insane, young man? Is it because of my demeanor? Because you see me calmly accepting your presence in my house? What else might I do? And what would it matter? Very shortly, Mr. Logan—maybe even within the next few minutes—this entire reality will cease to exist. We may be part of the reality that replaces it, you and I, but we won't be here. We will never have known each other. It will be a very different world. I have seen to that. Now all I have to do is wait."

Sadly, Logan gazed at the old man, then turned away. "You are insane," he repeated. "I've seen your utopia, Aleksei. Very tidy, very orderly. But there is no sanity in it. History didn't go that way, and it won't change now. You can't reach Josef Stalin. You can't reach anybody, anymore. Your great scheme has failed, Aleksei. You've played all your cards, and lost."

The shawl drew tighter around withered shoulders, and Logan knew at a glance that he had scored. The old man's eyes glared at him now with a fire that was pure hatred. It was time to push. "I only need to decide what to do with you, now," he said. "An asylum, possibly? But you're too old to rehabilitate, aren't you. Well, I suppose we can find a prison somewhere with a geriatric cell— "

Aleksei's cry was a hiss of rage. The shawl fell away, and a shaking, skeletal hand leveled a pistol at Logan. The timecop smiled sympathetically, then with a motion so quick that Aleksei hardly saw it, he ducked to the side, lunged, and wrenched the gun from the old man's fingers.

"Insane," Logan repeated. He removed the gun's loads and tossed it onto the desk. "Hopelessly insane."

"I am not insane!" Aleksei shrieked. "You'll see! Any moment now, this won't exist! Just wait!"

Logan shook his head. Casually, he walked once around the gold room, gazing at each of its glittering displays. Minutes passed, then more minutes. Finally Logan returned to the desk and leaned there.

Aleksei had the gun again, fumbling to place a cartridge in its action. Logan let him keep it. "Wait, Aleksei? How long? You know by now that you've failed. What did you do, send someone to eliminate Stalin? Stella Raines again, maybe? But she tried before, and failed. And now she's failed again. Sorry about that."

"No!" Aleksei raged. "No! This time I sent Vassili! Vassili never fails!"

"Vassili, huh?" Logan shrugged, recalling a captured time jumper's mention of the huge, silent man who was always at Aleksei's side. So it was Vassili the old man turned to, in desperation. Logan wondered idly who at TEC had been given the assignment to handle that ripple. To the old man, though, he said only, "Well, about now I suspect your Vassili is being hauled up before Timecourt. You won't see him again. Now, about yourself—"

"You will pay for this, Jack Logan!" Aleksei waved the gun wildly, not even trying to point it at Logan. "Stella knows you. She's expecting you! She will kill you, Logan. I have ordered it."

Logan grinned. "Stella's a big girl. Big enough to make her own decisions. Somehow I don't think you pay her enough to make her go down with a sinking ship. But we can ask her about it, if you like. Where is she?"

"Nebraska!" Aleksei shrilled. "Another time, but she'll be back. Be warned, Jack Logan! If this reality remains, and you are still alive, Stella will find you!"

"I don't think I'll lose sleep about that," Logan drawled. "Good employees are hard to find, if there's nobody left to pay them."

Aleksei hissed like an ancient snake. "She isn't my employee, you fool! She's my granddaughter!"

As gently as possible, Logan removed the pistol from the old man's hand again and laid it on the desk. Then while Aleksei watched, helpless, he used the computer to sort and select the personal files. Those dealing with Dosvestia, time travel, Aleksei's memoirs, and Am-Can's secret research he transmitted to Charles Graham's personal account at NSA. When the transmission was done, he placed a line call to TEC, coding his message by keypad.

"I'm counting on you, Taffy," he muttered.

Returning to the computer, he carefully deleted everything that had gone out, reformatting whole sections of memory to make sure that nothing remained. What was left, he put on open transmission to the RCMP and Interpol, then closed the computer down and disconnected its power. He cut the telephone cables, reversed polarity in the gold room's electric heating grid to send a dead short into the house's fuse boxes, and everything went out.

The house was dead, and it would take at least a new fuse box to ever resurrect it.

Finally, he turned again to the fuming old man. "I'm still waiting for the world to end, Aleksei. But it doesn't seem to be happening. Maybe some other time. Don't make any big plans for the future, though. The police will be here shortly, and I'm sure they'll arrange your future for you."

Not looking back, Logan strode from the now-shadowy gold room. He was halfway down the curving staircase when a single gunshot rang and echoed, from above.

Alex Porter—Aleksei Portenov—had decided not to wait around for the world to end.

Logan didn't try to retrace his steps into Am-Can. Instead, he went straight to Porter Tower, where he rode the enclosed tram down to Eaton Center. Striding through the sprawling ways of the big mall, he found the place with the steak sandwiches and ate another one.

When enough time had passed, he found the sublevel elevators and descended to Am-Can's research center. Claire Hemmings was waiting for him when he stepped out, and this time she wore no disguise. Her TEC uniform bore all of its proper insignia, and she handed Logan his.

"Put it on," she said. "I don't know what all you sent to Charles Graham, but there have been some serious strings pulled. We're here officially now, with the prime minister's blessing."

"They know about TEC?"

"Of course not. But they know we're specialists in something, and we belong here. I've seen a dozen white suits hauled out of there by red coats, in the twenty minutes I've waited here. Where were you?"

"I stopped for a sandwich." He grinned. "Real beef. Does your presence here mean they trust me with a time machine, now?"

"Trust you? I don't know. Maybe I'm here because they

don't." She glared at him, combative as usual, then her gaze softened. "We had reason to worry, you know. I mean, who knows what any of us would do, if we'd lost our whole world and all we had to do to get it back was . . . Well, I'm glad you're back, Logan. We all are."

The reserved, frosty mask of his face seemed about to soften, but then he looked away. "Don't ever count your chickens, Hemmings. Let's just get on with this job. Did they get Vassili?"

"They got him. He was trying to assassinate Stalin, but they intervened. A real clean bust. O'Donnelly got the collar."

"O'Donnelly? O'Donnelly's a historian, for God's sake! Who did he launch with?"

"Julie. They were all we had."

"A cyberpunk and a cheerleader," Logan muttered. "My God!"

Hemmings nodded vigorously. "Amen," she said. "Okay, I brought the vectors you wanted. ChronComp picked them up off Am-Can's launch records. Where are we going?"

"Nebraska," he said. "Nebraska in 1971. I'm going after Stella."

Beatrice, Nebraska
1971

It was nearly dark when Harry Sheffield pulled into the driveway. An inch of fresh snow had fallen during the day, and it crunched under the tires as he pulled up to the porch walk. He killed the engine and nudged his wife. "We're home, doll," he said. "Should I put the car away?"

"It'll still be here in the morning." Kaki yawned.

As they slid out of the car, she turned to gaze across the street. There were lights on in Jane's house, but the windows over the garage were dark.

Harry hauled out their suitcase and started up the steps. "Somebody's been here," he said, noting tracks in the snow.

He reached for his key, and Kaki was beside him, gripping his arm.

"Harry, wait!" she whispered. "Look."

The tracks led up the steps, to the front door, but there they ended. There were no tracks going away.

Forty-one years had passed since the last time Kaki Boyer had worn the uniform of the Time Enforcement Commission. She had been twenty years old then, a highly trained, sharp-eyed rookie officer with the world's most professional, most exclusive, and most secret policing agency. Now she was past sixty and thoroughly immersed in a different life in a different time. Forty-one years of adaptation—but still something remained. Like a lingering sixth sense, the footprints in the snow, there on the front porch, raised an old flag for her, and she hesitated. There was something wrong. The wind had calmed, and for an instant she thought there was a faint scent of gas.

But for Harry, the tracks were just tracks. He put his key in the lock and turned it. "Just one of the neighbors," he said. "They'll be back."

"Just wait a minute, will you?" Kaki urged. "There's something—"

But it was too late. Harry pushed the door open and went inside. Alert and nervous, Kaki followed, and he closed the door behind them. The low lights they had left were still on, and the living room was just as they had left it . . . almost. But now, inside, the smell of gas was much stronger. Harry noticed it then, too.

"We've got a leak," he said. "Don't touch any switches till we check it out."

He set down the suitcase, and Kaki saw what was different in the house. The sliding door to the kitchen was closed.

"Harry, wait," she said, but her husband was already heading for the kitchen. Just as he reached for the latch to open the door, Kaki saw the trap—a tiny patch of gray near the top of the door, with a hair-fine wire running from it to the frame. It was not a thing of this time, but it was something she recognized—a deadly trip-wire fuse, already triggered. The countdown had begun when the front door was opened, and the bomb was her kitchen. With a stifled scream, Kaki lunged across the room and grabbed Harry's arm, trying to pull him back.

Joe Brimmage was just driving by, on his way home from the new bakery west of town, when the Sheffield house blew up. With a deafening roar, the entire front of the house exploded outward, engulfing everything inside and for thirty feet outward—halfway to the street—in raging, killing flames.

Am-Can Timebase
2008

"So you pair are the American 'experts' we're supposed to assist?" The professional suspicion in Sergeant Inspector Colin Terrell's narrowed eyes betrayed the civil smile on his weathered face. He glanced at their proffered credentials, then looked them both up and down. "And might I ask what it is you're expert at?"

Logan returned the gaze, stare for stare. "We are expert at what we're dealing with here, Inspector. You've received orders?"

"You know bloody well I have, Agent Logan." Terrell bristled. "I'm to cordon this area and seal off everything beyond these doors. Everything yonder—" He indicated the triplex viewport a few feet away. "—is off limits to everybody."

"That's right." Logan nodded. "Just the two of us go in there. Nobody—and that means nobody—else."

"Right," Terrell rumbled. "But I'd be a bit more content if I had a few specifics. What is this we're dealing with, as you say? Terrorists? A bomb, maybe? A chemical weapon?

Can't see a bloody thing from that port except laboratories and a tunnel. What is it in there?"

"Nothing like that, Inspector," Claire Hemmings assured him. "It's just some technological research that our two governments want checked out. We're here to do that."

"Fat lot that tells me, miss." The policeman's tone softened, in deference to the lady, but the steel remained in his eyes. "How can I cordon a site, and avoid putting any of my people in jeopardy, if I don't know the dangers?"

Logan looked around him thoughtfully, at the stark white walls of this subterranean place; at the closed, massive doors where two red-coated Mounties stood stolid guard while uniformed urban police patrolled the corridors; at the little triplex observation port with its puzzling almost-view of the sled bay.

A saturnine grin touched his cheeks as he looked back at the chief inspector. "That's a fair question," he admitted, "and it deserves an answer. This is top secret, Inspector. We suspect unauthorized temporization, and we're here to check it out."

"Unauthorized . . . What?"

"It means time travel," Logan said blandly. "We have reason to think there's a time machine inside there, and we're here to investigate. We wouldn't want people jumping around in time without regard for regulations, would we?"

Terrell stared at him, his eyes narrowing even more.

"I mean, how would we set our watches if somebody bumped Greenwich Standard askew?" Logan pressed.

Terrell shook his head and looked away. "Bloody Yanks," he muttered. "Ask a simple, civil question—"

"Don't worry," Claire said. "Nothing's going to blow up or leak out or run amok when we go in there. All we need from you is to make sure nobody else goes in or comes out until we've finished."

The Am-Can timesled and its controls were almost identical to TEC's. Obviously, it was a copy from very complete plans.

"So much for the world's best-kept secret," Logan growled as Claire tested the timefield circuits and programmed in the vectors ChronComp had computed.

"Don't be so glum," she chided. "It was one U.S. senator. And by now he's so deep in Timecourt's jurisdiction, he'll never see daylight again."

"One senator," he muttered. "Sure. That only leaves about six hundred legislators to wonder about."

"Logan, you have to trust somebody!"

"I'd like to be a little more selective about trust," he grumbled. "To begin with, a legislator had to be a politician first to ever get elected. And most politicians start out as lawyers."

"Oh, shut up, Logan," Claire snapped. "You're making me as paranoid as you are." She completed her programming and sighed. "There. That's the best launch we're going to get. It's a little iffy, though. ChronComp had to estimate spatial vectors from Toronto, and I had to build in the time factor from here. We launch in five, and I gave us a thirty-minute window on your calculations. It's the best we can do without E-warp."

"Then stay close to that screen when I launch." Logan pointed. "At least you'll have manual override out to half Q."

"To hell with that!" Her eyes blazed as she looked up at him. "You're not launching alone this time. I'm going with you!"

"Oh?" His grin was pure ice. "And what's all that business about trust?"

"This is not negotiable, Logan."

"Then you'll have to program all the controls over to the sled's systems. There won't be anybody in the booth to kick us off."

"I've already done it," she said smugly. "Let's go, Logan. We launch in four and counting."

The sled track was a tunnel—a long, dark tube that once had seen subway trains but now was reinforced and vastly modified to serve a timesled. As they strapped in, Claire said nervously, "I can't even see the timefield from here. Just a long, dark hole."

"We'll see it in a minute," Logan assured her. "If it's any comfort, just think of it as the last thing you'll ever see if this bullet doesn't reach Q-velocity."

Claire took a deep breath. "Thanks," she growled. "I needed that."

In the front seat, Logan flipped switches, and the sled's console came to life. He ran a quick systems check, counting the seconds in his mind as the lights in front of him ticked them off. At the yellow, he threw the tachyon release, and the sled thundered as mighty drives erupted in its tail.

"Ten seconds to launch," he counted. " . . . seven . . . six . . . five . . . four . . . " He pushed the manual advance home, and the sled's autos took over, responding to the programming in Am-Can's linked system. " . . . three . . . two . . . one . . . " It was like being shot from a gun. Released, the tachyon drives thundered and heaved, inconceivable power slapping the sled down the tunnel at doubling and quadrupling Gs. The first three lighted counters were discernable as they passed, the rest a flitting blur. Ahead—cramped and massive in the confines of the tunnel—great armatures flared as three parts of a wormhole timefield flashed into existence.

Barely conscious against massive acceleration, Logan noted the velocity readings before him: 1814 . . . 1991 . . . 2283 . . . 2705 . . . 2921 . . . 2994! As the timefield flared open to receive it, the timesled hurtled into a nothingness beyond human comprehension—dimensions that could never be seen or truly understood.

Logan hit the ground hard and rolled, coming up against a drifted-over fence full of barbed wire, icy tumbleweeds, and pheasants. Startled birdcalls clucked and shrilled all around him, and flogging wings beat the air. Somewhere there were excited voices. As he rolled over, something struggled beneath him and pulled free. For an instant, angry bird eyes were an inch from his. Then in a flurry of furious wings, the pheasant spurred his cheek and took to the air.

Gunshots roared, and loads of birdshot whisked over his head. He ducked, rolled, and came to his feet, his gun out and ready.

Fifty feet away, four men with earmuff caps and shotguns gaped at him, lowering their guns as he stepped closer.

"Jesus, man," one of them gurgled, "sorry 'bout that. We didn't see you there."

"Well, you do now."

Logan wiped blood from the scratch beneath his eye

and looked around. It was an open hillside, in early dusk. Cold wind rattled leafless branches of a few low trees not far away, and there were wind drifts of snow.

"Which way to Beatrice?" he demanded.

One of the men pointed, hesitantly. "Town's just over there," he said. "'Bout eight miles."

"You, uh . . . you walkin' to Beatrice?" another asked. Then, noticing the odd attire of this apparition, "What are you, a game warden or something?"

Behind them, at the crest of the hill, a small figure appeared, waving. "Logan! Up here! What's keeping you?"

"Whatever he is," one of the hunters said to another, "there's two of 'em. He brought his missus along."

Eight miles, Logan thought. Well, so much for estimated spatial vectors.

Beatrice, Nebraska
1971

They rode the eight miles in the open bed of a Dodge pickup, and when they piled out at a quiet street corner, they heard one of their escorts mutter, "You better think of something to tell your wife, Jake. She's expecting pheasants, and she sure ain't gonna believe this story."

It was full evening when they found the house, the dusk deepening toward dark. From ChronComp's perusal of census data, they found the house Logan was looking for. But it was obvious there was no one home.

From the shadows of a winter-bare hedge line, they surveyed the place. "Now what?" Claire asked, breathing into cupped hands. The thermals in their jumpsuits did little for heads and hands, and it was cold.

"Let's scout it," Logan said. "Stella is around here, somewhere. You scout the street. I'm going for a closer look at the house."

Keeping to shadows, he sprinted across a neighboring lawn and around to the back of the Sheffield house. By neighborhood light he circled halfway around the house, pausing at windows to glance inside. Low lights were on in the living room and a high-windowed bathroom, but there was no sign of occupancy. The back quarter of the house—the kitchen and utility section—was dark. He was at the rear of the house when the evening wind calmed for a moment, and his nostrils twitched. He smelled gas—the distinctive, skunklike aroma of commercial natural gas odorized by additives.

And the screen-porch door was slightly ajar. Moving soundlessly, he mounted the steps, slipped in, and tried the back door. It opened when he turned its knob.

Just beyond was a partial hallway—utility room on one side, tool room on the other. The odor was strong here. Using his little pocket light, he glanced around the two rooms, looking for a source. Directly ahead, the hall turned to the left past a solid-looking closed door. He glanced down the left hall, then opened the door a crack. Gas and skunk odor assailed him. The kitchen was full of it. And in that instant he saw the booby trap—a twenty-first-century hair-wire detonator at the far kitchen door, triggered and ready. Holding his breath, he aimed his light across, narrowing the beam. The detonator was time-set. Somewhere beyond was a relay that would set it off. Thirty seconds later, this kitchen would become a firebomb.

Carefully, Logan closed the door. He was turning to leave when light from outside flooded through the left hall. Beyond was a carpeted studio—sound equipment arrayed around a grand piano—and through its windows he saw a car in the driveway, with people getting out, heading for the house. As he glimpsed them, they disappeared from his line of sight.

Intuition—or hunch—drew Logan's glance across the studio to the open doors there. Beyond was a stairwell, a little foyer, and what must be a living room with low lights aglow. He circled the piano and was heading for the foyer when the front door opened and he heard people coming in.

And in the instant of the door opening, he heard a faint click elsewhere . . . the deadly little sound of a hair-wire detonator being activated.

"We've got a leak," a man's voice said. "Don't touch any switches till we check it out."

Then a woman's voice. "Harry, wait!"

As Logan came around the stairwell, there was a stifled scream. A small, agile woman was grappling with a tall, white-haired man, pulling him back.

And in a rush of memory, Logan recognized the woman. She was much older now, but he knew her. "Kaki!" he shouted. "This way!"

He caught each of them by a sleeve, thrusting them toward the protective stairwell and the windows beyond. The bay window over the driveway bulged out and shattered as he plunged backward through it, his arms wrapped around the two old people, protecting them as best he could from the glass and the fall.

They tumbled through, and behind them a deafening roar erupted. Gushing, billowing flame followed them out the window, rolling over them as they fell into the scratching arms of a spirea hedge just below.

For an instant they lay in a sprawled heap, stunned by the impact. Then they struggled upright, and Logan half dragged the pair across the driveway to fall with them behind the car parked there.

A few yards away windows shattered, walls thrummed, and white-hot flame thundered outward.

In the flaring, flickering light of rising flames, the old man groaned and sat up. "Good Lord," he breathed. "Kaki, are you all right?"

The gray-haired woman nodded and pulled him close, hugging him. Over his shoulder, she stared at the time-cop. "Logan?" she whispered. "You—you are Jack Logan, aren't you? I remember you."

"It's about time somebody did," Logan muttered. "Hello, Kaki. I've been looking for you. Sorry about your house. Do you know who did this?"

"It was Stella," Kaki Boyer Sheffield sobbed, raising her head to see the inferno that had been her home. "Stella Raines . . . from TEC! She's here, in this time. But—but why? Why would she . . . do a thing like this?"

Sirens were wailing somewhere, and there were people on the street, gawking at the blaze. Logan helped the Sheffields to the safety of a neighbor's lawn, and Claire Hemmings appeared beside them. The blond systems analyst had blood dripping down her chin, and her left eye was swollen almost shut. "I found her, Logan," she gasped. "Across the street. She was watching."

Logan touched her bruised cheek with gentle fingers.

"You look like hell, Taffy," he said. "It's a wonder she didn't kill you."

"I was lucky." Claire shrugged painfully. "I saw her first. I grabbed and ran . . . God, but that woman can hit! I thought she'd come after me, but then there were people all over. I guess she didn't know she'd lost this." Claire opened her fist to reveal a little trinket that might have been a pendant or locket, but wasn't. It was a temporal retrieval unit, Am-Can design.

The sirens were closer now. Kaki clung to her husband's arm and stared at the two timecops. A tear crept down her cheek, leaving a tiny path in the soot smudge there. She looked from one to the other of them, her eyes pausing at the TEC insignia on the dark uniforms. "I—I guess I have to go back now?"

"You swore an oath when you joined TEC," Logan growled. "Do you remember it?"

"Every word of it." She lowered her eyes. "And I've never broken it."

"And you know the procedure now?"

"Leave no tracks." She nodded. "I know."

Harry Sheffield glared at the TEC cops, ready to fight them if he had to.

"Then, attend to this situation, Agent Boyer," Logan ordered, indicating the burning house. "We'll talk later."

On a cold, blustery morning, Jack Logan and Claire Hemmings interrogated Harry and Kaki Sheffield in a neat room at the Holiday Villa. Logan asked the questions, and Hemmings listened. Faintly, in the background, a radio emitted selections from *Fiddler on the Roof*.

"Yours?" Claire had asked Harry.

The composer shook his head. "Wish it were," he said. "All I contributed was some bridging. But it's pretty, isn't it?"

Now Logan tried to piece together a puzzle that had begun several weeks ago for him, but more than forty years ago for them.

"So that was you I saw that day, in 1930 New York," Kaki said. "I was never sure. I just saw a TEC jumpsuit, and I panicked."

"Why?"

"A lot of reasons, I guess. What I was looking for there, on that building site, wasn't mine. It wasn't anybody else's, either, and I knew it would never be found historically, but that didn't make it mine."

"The gold coins, you mean."

"Yeah. I knew they were there. I saw them on my first mission. Maybe I was feeling guilty about wanting to take them. Or maybe when I saw a TEC uniform, I just realized how much I didn't want to go back to my own time. Anyhow, I panicked. Then a policeman chased me, and I ran, and something fell on me and hurt my arm."

"But you did take the coins."

"I went back later and got them."

"And you sold them in Toronto."

"Yeah." She gazed fondly at Harry. "That was some time later. Actually, we never used very much of the money, but just knowing we had it—"

"It gave us courage," Harry Sheffield continued. "It gave me the backbone to finally break loose from the crummy dives and do what I always wanted to do. Knowing we had something to fall back on . . . well, it made us brave."

"And being brave made us lucky," Kaki said. "Even if I have to go back now, even if it's over—" She took Harry's hand for a gentle squeeze. "—I wouldn't have traded a minute of it."

Logan paced the room, twice across and twice back, deep in thought. Then he turned. "Why should you go back, Kaki?"

"Logan!" Claire snapped. "Don't play games. Of course we have to take her in."

"On what charge?"

Claire stared at him, not believing what she heard. "Because she's a paradox!" she said. "She doesn't belong in this time!"

"I'm a paradox, too," he reminded her. "I don't even belong in my own time, but I'm here. As to Mrs. Sheffield, I don't see where she's broken any laws."

"Dereliction of—" Claire came to her feet. "Would you people excuse us for a moment, please?" She grabbed Logan's arm and herded him out of the room, into the hall. "Dereliction of duty," she continued. "Failure to respond to a legal summons. Evading arrest! Not to mention manipulation of history for personal gain—"

Logan shook his head. "Oh, come on, Hemmings! Dereliction? She was marooned in 1929, through circumstances beyond her control—"

"I'd have retrieved if I could," Kaki assured them, through the open door. "But my unit was gone."

Logan glanced around, frowning at the interruption, then closed the door and continued. "And failure to respond? Hemmings, the missing-agent bulletin never went beyond TEC. You know that. And even if she'd known about it, she couldn't respond. She was stuck in a past time."

Hemmings glared up at him, as nose-to-nose as his twelve-inch height advantage allowed. "Evading arrest, then!"

"Are you talking about that aborted launch, to Beatrice? ChronComp wouldn't vector that launch, remember? That's why we had to launch from a bootleg facility, because TEC's own big brain refused to intervene here. Maybe we ought to arrest ChronComp."

The room door opened again, just a bit. Still glaring at each other, Logan and Hemmings reached out simultaneously to sieze its handle and close it firmly.

"She's a TEC agent out of time!" Claire insisted. "She's an anachronism. Maybe a dangerous one."

"The anachronism was the coins, not Kaki," Logan pointed out. "None of the incidents track back to her, do they? What it comes down to is whether Agent Boyer in any way caused the anachronisms that began on May 12, 1930. As far as I can see, she's clean. So she recovered those Revolutionary coins. They weren't on anybody's historical slate to begin with. What's her crime, Hemmings? Trespassing?"

Hemmings fumed, but she kept her tone level. "Logan, you know as well as I do that there's nothing right about a TEC agent just—just staying in the past and not coming back. I say we retrieve her at least for questioning."

"Retrieve her to where? Toronto? Be realistic, Hemmings. If TEC's artificial intelligences won't intervene in this matter, there has to be a reason."

"So what do you think we should do?"

"What we came for," he said. "We came after Stella

Raines. We don't have her yet. Let's concentrate on that, for the time being."

The door opened behind them, and Kaki peered out, apologetically.

"You two ought to clarify your relationship," she said. "With that level of hostility, you might discover that you're in love. But I think I know why your machines balked at sending a time mission to intervene in our lives. It's our son, Jimmy. He's just now inventing E-warp, out in Colorado. I'm sure ChronComp has fail-safes to protect the existence of its own components."

Now they looked at her, aghast. "E-warp?"

"We could have some coffee sent up," Harry suggested. "They have room service here."

XIII

"It's a fail-safe," Bob O'Donnelly said, depositing several erratic pounds of printout on Eugene Matuzek's desk. "We knew ChronComp had an elaborate fail-safe system, but tracking it is like unraveling a hooraw's nest. It took S and R two days just to find the operative code. But they found it. It's 'MOTHER HEN.' It's why the system balks at vectoring a launch to the proximity of Beatrice, Nebraska. ChronComp is protecting its sources."

Matuzek gazed at the huge stack of equations. "Why did you bring me all this, Bob? Just tell me what it means."

O'Donnelly brushed back a lock of unruly hair. "It means ChronComp is programmed to protect the origins of all of its components. Real clever, for a system dealing with time travel. It has a hard-data file on every part of itself, and on every event sequence that produced any of its components. It is programmed not to allow interference with its own technological background, or any of TEC's hardware."

Matuzek raised a quizzical eyebrow.

216

"It's simple." O'Donnelly shrugged. "If we tried to, say, initiate a launch that might jeopardize Hans Kleindast's invention of time travel, ChronComp wouldn't let us. Same with the Dome, the wormhole-effect four-dimensional field, any of the technologies involved in temporal displacement. In this case, it might be protecting the discovery of eventuality-wave resonance patterns."

"E-warp?"

"Right. The E-warp principle was discovered in the 1970s by a research team in Colorado, funded through NSA. One of the team members was Dr. James Henry Sheffield. From Beatrice, Nebraska."

In the library that served as his office, Dale Easter, chief of TEC's historical staff, put down a newspaper and picked up another one from the stack. The *Beatrice Daily Sun*, more than thirty years ago, had been a small paper serving a small town, and gleaning through its columns was dull work. Things had happened in Beatrice in late 1971, of course. Things happen everywhere, every day. But Easter was looking for references to anyone named Sheffield or anything that might have anything to do with the mysterious mission ChronComp had vectored for a timesled six hundred miles away in Toronto.

Claire Hemmings had jumped from Toronto to 1971 Beatrice, Nebraska, and the paradoxer Logan was with her. They were looking for a rogue time jumper called Stella Raines.

The *Beatrice Daily Sun*'s November 22, 1971, edition lay before his tired eyes, and he scanned the local headlines. A city employee was being investigated for improper use of city equipment. Workers at a packing plant were threatening to strike. The Methodist Ladies' Auxiliary was collecting blankets for the needy. A sportsmen's group was lobbying in Lincoln for an extended deer season . . . the usual news of a little town.

Easter yawned, took off his glasses, and rubbed his eyes . . . then blinked and gasped as the page before him swam and blurred. He blinked again, put his glasses on, and peered at the paper. The Methodist Ladies were gone, and the impending strike was in a lower position. Now there was a story about a house fire. He read the lead, then grabbed the paper and headed for the captain's office.

The home of Harry and Mary Katherine Sheffield had been destroyed by a gas-leak explosion and fire. The occupants, just returning from a visit to Colorado, had narrowly escaped injury.

Beatrice, Nebraska
1971

In the coffee shop of the Paddock Hotel, Stella Raines put down the latest *Sun* and leaned back, gazing out the front window at a new day. The house had burned, but the Sheffields had escaped, and Stella knew how. TEC— the time police! They were here. The little blonde who now had her retrieval unit was TEC, and Stella had a feeling there was another, too—the man called Logan.

Without her retrieve, Stella Ilyanova Raines was trapped in this time, and her mission was unfinished.

Kill Logan, her grandfather had said. If he interferes again, kill him. Beneath her white fur coat, Stella felt the comforting pressure of the pistol Aleksei had given her. It rested in its holster beside her left breast, reminding her with every breath.

Fifteen years ago, there had been killing pain there. She had been in London then, just beginning her service with Scotland Yard. The bullet had come from nowhere, and she remembered nothing after that except a blur of bright lights, busy people working around her, then a clergyman saying a prayer.

But then, somehow, she had other attention, and through it she heard the words "Spare no expense. This is Alex Porter's granddaughter."

And in that moment, suspended between life and death, Stella had made a vow. Whatever her grandfather asked of her, no matter what, she would never hesitate.

Yet now she had failed him for a third time. Once again, the people with the TEC emblem had intervened, and now she knew from the newspaper that the Sheffield couple still lived.

She finished her coffee, observing the comings and goings of people. They came in all shapes and sizes, and they came and went as people do, on the myriad business of their time. The pace of life was leisurely, the little courtesies easier and the comfort zones wider than she was used to. The small-town scene only emphasized the obvious. There weren't as many people in this world as there would be in 2008, and their variety seemed accentuated by that fact.

Idly, she noticed a teenage boy with a stack of handbills. He came in from the street, pink-cheeked with the cold, and spoke for a moment to one of the waitresses. He handed her a handbill, then left. Stella watched the girl cross to the front window and post the notice there, in a corner of the glass that already held a dozen other posters.

The girl turned, paused, and smiled. "Somebody's trying to apologize to somebody, I guess," she said. "You know anybody named Stella?"

"Yes—" She tensed. "—I probably do."

"Oh, good!" The girl giggled. "Well, it looks like her boyfriend wants to change his ways." She indicated the poster in the window. "One of the McDonald boys left this. He had a whole stack of them. I guess they're leaving them all over town."

"Must be important," Stella muttered. She tipped the surprised girl a dollar and went out to the street. The note in the window was an offset reproduction—in the idiom of the time, a Xerox copy.

"Stella—" it read. "It's over. Talk to me. —Logan."

"Over?" Stella murmured. "No, Logan. It isn't over. I haven't finished yet."

Leaving Claire to look after the Sheffields, Logan went scouting. Even in a little town, there are a thousand places to hide, and his chance of finding Stella Raines before she wanted to be found was remote. He would have to bring her to him. His method was a note, reproduced at a local copy shop and enthusiastically circulated by a pair of local boys who sometimes tended the Sheffields' lawn. It would get to her, he knew. Then it would be up to Stella.

Now he needed to be seen, to establish a meeting ground. And he needed to know the lay of the land. He acquired a long overcoat, snow boots, and a wool cap, and spent a time roving the streets of Beatrice.

There was an old, brick-walled packing company building down by the river, that Kaki had suggested. It was three stories tall, deserted but still sound, well back from the active parts of town—the kind of abandoned place everybody sees every day but no one really notices. He looked it over, forced his way inside, and climbed to the top, then to the roof. Once there, he discarded his disguise and strolled around for a few minutes, in full view of anybody watching.

The invitation . . . and the meeting place. Now he would give her time for her move.

For a while he prowled around the quiet residential area where the remains of the burned house were being stared at, poked into, and photographed by various people, and he had a look at the upstairs garage apartment across the street, where Stella had been.

Stella Raines was a professional, he noticed. A few garments still hung in the closet—virtually everything white—and some lingerie in a dresser drawer, but she had left nothing in the place to help anyone find her or even identify her . . . nothing except a small, white foam-plastic mold in a trash can, that Logan recognized as a shell box. It had once contained fifty nine-millimeter cartridges, and the little indentations left by the bullets were not quite like any bullets known in 1971.

"Teflon," he mused. "We're getting serious now, aren't we, Stella? Well, so much for flakwear."

Logan didn't want to underestimate Stella Raines. She wasn't TEC, but another version of her—the Stella he knew from another reality—had been. And that meant the best of the best. Stella—a Stella without oath of office, without the rigid code of honor of the law enforcement profession—could be deadly.

At a little place downtown, he stopped for a beef sandwich.

When he estimated that enough time had passed, Logan returned to the old brick building by the river. Setting aside his camouflage garments, he approached openly, in plain sight, along a weedy, overgrown railroad spur flanked by runs of crusted snow. His eyes were in constant motion, scanning every feature of the building and its surroundings. The nearer he approached, the better target he became. But it was time to find out if Stella was willing to talk.

Stella saw Logan almost as soon as he left the Holiday Villa, and she watched him walking along the street. Logically, she knew he was hunting her, but something—some sixth sense—told her that he was trying to set up a meeting. She had met him, she had fought him, and she knew his mind. He was good, and he could be dangerous. But there was something puzzling about him. He was, somehow, a man of another time, of a slightly different culture.

Old-fashioned values, she thought. Right for right's sake. Benefit of the doubt, all that. Like a movie hero from the 1950s, he would do what he said he would do. The open message on the coffee shop window meant exactly what it said: He wanted to talk.

Stella tailed him, waiting. And when he paused, then turned at an old gravel street and headed for the abandoned packing house, she knew he was selecting a meeting place.

From the cover of a storefront, she saw him emerge atop the building, coatless now and clad in the dark uniform of TEC.

He's advertising, she thought. He's showing me where he will be. Now he will allow an hour or so for me to think it over.

"I'll meet you there, Logan," Stella murmured. "But first I will do what I was sent to do."

Turning, she retraced her steps to the Holiday Villa. Harry Sheffield's car was in the parking lot, and there was no one around. It took only a few minutes to walk to the Standard Oil station at the next corner, slip in and out unobserved, and return to the motel with a large, mechanic's coverall and a handful of tools.

She slid under the car, used the tools she had brought, then returned to the service station and snapped the lock on the women's restroom. Her own clothing was still there, where she had left it.

From a public telephone in the lobby of the Villa, she placed a call to Harry Sheffield's room.

Kaki answered the call. "Mrs. Sheffield?" a woman's voice inquired. "Mrs. Sheffield, this is Ann Johnson, Central States Gas. We're trying to help your local utility with its state report on your house fire last night. I understand there were no personal injuries . . . that you and your husband are all right?"

"Well, we're still kicking." Kaki sighed. "But our house isn't. It wasn't your fault, though. We're not blaming anybody. It was an accident. We've already discussed all this with the authorities."

"We appreciate that," the voice said. "But we have a . . . Well, you may have heard that our company is involved in hearings right now, for renewal of common carrier status, and this is quite a problem for us. Would you mind very much talking to one of our field people?"

"Of course not," Kaki said, glancing across the room at Claire Hemmings. The TEC agent and Harry were working the *Post* crossword puzzle. Kaki covered the phone's handset. "It's the gas company," she said. "They're in a tizzy about the fire."

Claire nodded, and Kaki told the caller, "I guess we could do that."

"Oh, that's fine," Ann Johnson assured her. "Mr. Mellett is in your area today. He's at Filley. I'll see if he can run over to Beatrice . . . unless it would be possible for you to meet him at Filley? He's doing inspections there."

Kaki hesitated, then said, "Oh, it's only ten miles. We'll just drive over there."

Across the room, Claire sat bolt upright, turning startled eyes toward her. Kaki frowned and put a finger to her lips. "No, that's just fine," she told the caller. "Where? Yes, no problem. Tell him we'll be there in about an hour."

She hung up, and Claire erupted. "You're not going anywhere! We're waiting right here for Logan!"

"Hon, somebody just tried to kill us," Harry chimed in. "We're not leaving this room till—"

"Oh, hush, both of you!" Kaki crossed to the window, eased the blind slightly, and peered outside. "Do you think I'm an imbecile, for God's sake? That wasn't any gas company. They wouldn't run inspections at Filley. They'd be right here in Beatrice. Besides, that call came from right here in the motel. I imagine that was Stella, and she's trying to get us out on the road."

Claire gazed at the aging woman with sudden respect. "You really were a timecop, weren't you!"

Stella left the motel by a side door, away from the parking lot and the view of the facing rooms. She was less than satisfied with the arrangements for the Sheffields. The female TEC agent was still around somewhere, probably guarding them. And the ten-minute ignition blaster under the car's gas tank was slipshod at best. She had learned the trick from Irish free-state rebels in the nineties, and she had seen it fail as often as it succeeded. But it was the best she could do now, and time was running out. One of the TEC people—probably the man—had her retrieval unit, and she wanted it back.

A bank's time-temperature sign told her that an hour had passed since Logan's selection of the old brick building by the river. It was time to meet him there.

Approaching the boarded-up old building, Logan was wary. Stella Raines had carried no visible side arm on their two previous encounters, but now he knew she was armed, and the flak weave of his uniform wouldn't stop a Teflon-tipped cop-killer bullet.

Still, he reached the building without incident and ducked into the gloomy interior. Moving away from the breached doorway, he made a soundless circuit of the ground floor, then crouched in deep shadows.

He listened intently for a full minute and heard nothing but the rhythmic creak of weathered shutters where the cold breeze stroked them. Then, not moving, he called, "Stella! Stella Raines! I want to talk!"

Somewhere above, wood floors creaked and a deep, female voice said, "There's nothing to talk about, Logan. I have to kill you now."

Moving a few feet to the right, toward the side stairway, Logan let his ears guide him. She was almost directly overhead, but moving.

"Stella, your grandfather is dead," he called. "I didn't kill him. He killed himself. Dosvestia has failed. It's all over."

"You lie!" The voice came from farther left now. "My grandfather would never—"

"He used you, Stella! He sent you away, then he tried to change history so that you could never come back. There would be no place to come back to. He sent Vassili to kill Josef Stalin. Listen to me, Stella! He sent you into an anachronism that would have erased you if it had happened!"

There was a long silence, then rafters creaked and the voice above had shifted again. She's placing herself, Logan thought. She's getting ready for me to come up those stairs.

"This doesn't have to happen, Stella!" he called. "You can stop it right now. I'm telling the truth. The White Russia dream is ended. Aleksei Portenov is dead."

The silence this time was even longer, and when she spoke again, there was a tired acceptance in her tone that said she believed him. Believed him . . . but it made no difference.

"Who are you, Logan? What does *TEC* mean?"

"Time Enforcement Commission," he said. "I'm a policeman. A timecop."

He edged closer to the stairway, then ducked under it. Just beyond was an open chute, where a conveyor had stood. Making no sound, Logan stretched upward, grabbed a frame brace, and levered himself up through the hole.

Ten feet away was the head of the staircase where he had been. Three feet beyond, Stella Raines crouched in shadows, her back to him. Her gun was holstered.

"Logan," she called. "When we fought, I felt you knew me. How did you know me, Logan?"

He was directly behind her when he said, "From another life, Stella."

Her reaction was unbelievably swift. Like a spring uncoiled, she spun—not away, as most would have done, but directly toward him—and lashed out.

The kick would have broken bones, had it landed. But Logan wasn't there. As momentum carried her half-around, he hit the floor and rolled, knocking her pivot foot from beneath her. He tried for a shoulder hold, but it was like grappling with fog. She slammed her knuckles into his armpit, rattled his teeth with a dizzying chop, and danced away . . . directly into his stiff-arm thrust as he somersaulted to block her retreat.

She came up against a pillar and clung there for an instant. "You're good," she growled. "Where did you learn that?"

"From you, Stella." He circled, seeking an opening. "I told you, I knew you in another life. You were TEC, too. This is a different reality, Stella."

"In any other reality I'd be dead now! Aleksei saved my life!"

"In my reality you were a TEC expert. You taught cadets to defend themselves, and sometimes Karl Muller brought you flowers and took you dancing. This is what happens when history gets changed, Stella. It doesn't get better. It gets worse."

She came off the pillar like lightning striking, barely missing Logan with a crippling attack. He dodged, caught her with knuckles to the spine as she passed, and received bruised ribs in return. He veered away, gasping for breath. The woman was nearly as big as him, and unbelievably quick. And she knew every trick in the book.

But now she was worried, and it showed in her hesitation. When they came together again, Logan feinted, exposing his throat, giving her a target for a killing blow, but instead she sidestepped, going again for his sore ribs. The kick scored, and he scored, and they spun apart, circling like hunting cats. They were both bleeding now.

"Who's Karl Muller?" Stella panted.

Logan wiped blood from a cut above his eye. "A theoretician," he said. "A big, homely Dutchman with two kids—" He crouched, charged, stunned her left arm, and took a solid kick to the solar plexus in return. "—two kids," he gasped, backing away, "and no wife. Greta died in a traffic accident. Now Karl does his job, tends his flower garden, and collects pictures of sunsets."

"Who does he have, in—in this reality?"

"Nobody, Stella. You aren't there."

He braced himself for another attack, but instead she

backed away, and now there was a gun in her hand. "Stop it!" she hissed. "Just . . . stop it!"

Logan straightened, then stepped toward her. "You stop it, Stella," he said. "It's your call."

Claire Hemmings found the broken boards on the old building. She flattened herself against the brick wall, gun drawn, when she heard the sounds inside. Bright sunlight glinted on the little drifts of snow, and she closed her eyes for a moment, letting her pupils adjust, then swung around and leveled her gun toward the shadows inside.

"Hold your fire!" Logan's shout came from somewhere in the darkness. Then there was movement, and two figures emerged. Stella Raines's wrists were strapped in a come-along, and Logan walked a few steps behind her.

Claire frowned as they stepped out into the cold sunlight. "My God," she breathed. "Logan, you look like Sunday leftovers. You both do. What's going on?"

"We've been getting reacquainted." Logan shrugged, wincing at the motion. "Stella, this is Claire Hemmings. I believe you've met. Where are Kaki and Harry?"

"I left them with the local fire chief." Claire put her side arm away. "Nobody looks for anybody in a fire station. Okay, Logan, you've got your collar. What now?"

"Now we go home," he said. "I think we're done here."

"What about Kaki? We've got to do something about her."

"Why?" he drawled, tilting his head in challenge. "We don't have a single charge against her, and you know it.

And she's about as much a paradox in this time as the mayor of Beatrice is."

"But—"

"Drop it, Hemmings! Kaki Boyer retired a long time ago. Let's get out of her life now and let her live it."

"But she knows about time travel! They both do!"

"So does Albert Einstein," Logan snapped. "And so will a thousand or so other people in thirty-five years. So what? It's still a secret."

XIV

Sergeant Inspector Colin Terrell was in his office when his security detail called from Eaton Center. The Yanks were out of the flash tunnel in the sealed Am-Can lab. Two had gone in, and three came out. It took the inspector eleven minutes to get to the Am-Can installation.

In the subterranean corridor beneath Eaton Center, a pair of Mounties still stood guard at the off-limits door while several policemen gathered at the triplex viewport, peering through it. Terrell joined them. Beyond, in the closed laboratories, he could see three people—the two U.S. "experts" and a tall, blond woman in a white jump-suit. All three looked as though they had been through a major war. Even the little honey-blond expert was sporting a livid shiner.

"Have they come out?" Terrell demanded.

"No, sir," a policeman said, and shrugged. "There was another big flash down there where the tunnel begins, then those three came just strolling up through that decontamination chamber or whatever it is. Since then they've been playing with some computers or something. Shall we go in?"

"We shall not," Terrell growled. "We'll wait. But if they don't come out soon I may ring up the minister about special pay for aggravation."

"You've seen it all, now," Logan told Stella as the screens flicked off. "That's the kind of world Aleksei Portenov and Dosvestia envisioned. Do you like it?"

Stella Raines shook her head slowly, a shaken pallor enhancing the bruises on her handsome face. "It's awful," she murmured. "I never dreamed—"

"That world would have existed if you or Vassili had succeeded in eliminating Stalin," Claire said. "This is a valid scenario. Our own computers have verified it."

"It does exist," Stella said. "It isn't a replacement reality. It's a parallel reality. Don't you know eventuality theory?"

"I know there are theories." Claire nodded. "But nobody has ever tested them."

"They've been tested," Stella said. "What do you think all these facilities are for? Time travel? You know we don't need research scientists for that. It's accomplished technology. We only need technicians. No, eventuality theory has been researched, Agent Hemmings—right here at Am-Can. We've used timesled technology for controlled alterations, and traced them. There isn't just one time line. There is an infinite number, and every one—every possible history—exists somewhere in the spectrum."

Logan took a deep breath, then exhaled it slowly. "Then altering a time line doesn't destroy the future beyond it? It goes on?"

"It goes on." Stella nodded. "The alteration creates a branch—a new eventuality curve alongside it, and that becomes a history, too."

She stood, walked to a control panel, and activated a series of switches. Nearby, a section of wall slid away, exposing an exquisite diorama beyond—a miniature landscape over which artificial sunlight came and went, tiny winds blew, and little clouds of water vapor created miniature rainfalls.

"An artificial environment," Stella said. "Plants and some lower animal forms. There are fourteen charted histories within that tank—each one real, each one documented, and each current. We have a miniature timefield—microrobotics duplicating the timesled's function—to test every history by triangulated launch. The documentation is all on CW file here."

"All this," Claire breathed, looking back at the screens that had just shown them the utopia of the White Russian empire, "and Dosvestia wanted to go back to that?"

Logan paced a few steps, and back, deep in thought. "So an alteration just creates another history," he muttered. "Then what happens when an alteration is negated?"

Stella shrugged. "Then the gap is bridged. Both histories go on, but I suppose whoever unchanged the change goes back to the earlier branch. That gets into uncharted areas, Logan. There isn't any way to test it."

Claire stared at her partner. "Logan, are you thinking what I think you're thinking?"

"I think we've finished here," Logan said. "We'll let Charles Graham's masterminds sort it out with their Canadian buddies. I'm sure they'll find a place for Stella Raines, with all the research they have facing them."

"You can't do it, Logan! You can't just—"

He grinned at her, stepped close, and took her hand in a gentle grip. "How many times do I have to tell you, Hemmings? Trust me!"

Before she could react, his fingers went to the retrieval unit on her wrist and gripped its control. "I came to Toronto by packing crate, Taffy, but you came by time-launch. You're twelve hours out of sync, remember?"

With a quick twist, Logan activated the retrieve, then stepped back as the reality of Claire Hemmings swirled, coalesced, and collapsed into nothing. "Take care of yourself, Taffy," he murmured. "Have a nice history."

Stella gaped at him in disbelief. "You—you sent her back—"

"Just twelve hours," he said. "It was a conveyance jump, back to TEC. Now, let's get you into the proper hands, shall we?"

Carefully he removed her come-along, then took her by the arm and led her to the sealed door and opened it.

"Hello, Inspector," he said to the puzzled Terrell, just outside. "Good of you to meet us. This lady is Stella Ilyanova Raines. She's a Canadian citizen, in protective custody. She's yours now. Take good care of her. She's a very important witness."

Once again sealed inside Am-Can's laboratories, this time alone, Logan went to the timesled controls and programmed the field for autocontrol, just as Claire had taught him. The vectors were for Lower Manhattan Island, twelve hundred hours, twelve May, 1930.

New York City
1930

He landed tumbling, in the narrow, littered space between a tool shed and a latrine shack, and crouched there for a moment, getting his bearings. Then he stood and peered out, past rough-board corners. It was a construction site, no more than three acres in size and pocked with the pits and piles of unfinished footing excavations.

A barricade had been thrown up around the perimeter, and beyond it unruly mobs of men swarmed, shouting and gesturing, while police officers maintained a thin surveillance just inside.

Logan recognized the scene. He had been here before, and from his vantage between the shacks he could see the same pit where he had materialized—and fallen in— the last time he was here.

But it was an hour earlier now. The mob beyond the fence had not yet surged across it, and in that one pit, a small group of men worked with picks and shovels.

The trouble was concentrated on the north side of the site—an open area a hundred yards wide from the project fence to the soot-stained brick wall of an adjoining building. Scaffold ropes drooped from the roof of that building, and part of the wall was fresh-scrubbed and whitewashed.

Logan turned to look at the south boundary, where steel was rising for a tower that would be part of what was built here. Topmen, cut welders, and tappers were clambering into position there, while men on the ground prepared buckets of rivets to be hauled up to them.

Fixing the entire area in his mind, Logan left his cover and sprinted for the east fence. Dodging between surprised policemen, he jumped to the top of a pallet stack and vaulted over the fence to the street beyond. Here the crowd was not so thick or so boisterous, just a normal busy street where jitneys rolled and pedestrians jostled one another on the walks.

Drawing a few surprised stares, Logan pushed through the crowds northward, past the construction fence and the adjoining lot, then turned and ran along the side of the brick building there. Two painters and a roughneck in stained overalls were jockeying a scaffold onto its slings, hoisting it waist-high for loading.

Logan approached them, looked them over, and let them see the official-looking insignia on his launch suit and the gun at his hip.

"You men!" he ordered. "This is an emergency zone! Clear out!"

The roughneck backed away, then turned and ran. The two painters stared at the timecop.

"You heard me!" Logan snapped. "There's going to be trouble here. Don't you see it? Now get out of here! Come back later, when the fuss has died down!"

It was all the encouragement they needed. They turned and hurried away, and Logan watched them go. When they were out of sight, he adjusted the pulley slings on the scaffold and set a five-gallon bucket of white paint and a six-inch brush on its planks. Then he put on a drip coat over his uniform, climbed aboard, and began hauling the scaffold upward, end by end, a foot at a time. Fifteen feet above the ground, he cleated it off and went to work.

He had been at it for five minutes when a policeman hailed him from below. "You up there! What are you doing?"

Logan peered down at him and brandished his brush. "Painting a sign," he said.

"Well, get it done and stay out of the way!" the cop ordered. He waved a thumb toward the catcalling, angry mobs nearby. "Man could get hurt around here today."

"Be done in a little while," Logan assured him.

The job took twenty minutes. When it was finished, he lowered the scaffold, left the paint, brush, and coat where he had found them, and made his way down the street to a gap in the fence where a passing truck had turned wide and knocked a plank loose. He ducked through the opening, climbed to the flat roof of a site shed, and flattened himself there, staying out of sight.

Fifty yards away, the men were emerging from their pit, two of them carrying a greenish copper sea chest. A car was waiting for them at the far corner, and some of them loaded the chest into it and drove away. "Stuff belongs in a museum, not a free-for-all," one of the diggers shouted.

There were more police on the site now, a thin line of blue-coat authority facing the rioters across the fence while squads roamed the site, ready to back up the guards where they were needed.

Watching from atop the shed, Logan saw a familiar figure—a tall, husky young cop with unruly dark hair peeking from beneath his helmet. He was with a fresh squad coming in from an eastward precinct, and at the pit the sergeant in charge pointed at him. "This's your station, Johnny-O! Hold your ground an' keep your eyes open!"

As the squad hurried away, Johnny-O clambered to the top of the rubble heap beside the pit and stood there, feet spread wide, hands behind his back—a pose of authority, precisely by the book.

"A rookie," Logan mused, studying him. A good-looking kid, he thought. Solid and strong. But mostly he studied the face, and in it he saw a startling resemblance. Johnny-O, he noticed, looked a lot like himself. Now the hunch became a certainty. That rookie cop was John O'Hara . . . and John O'Hara was the source of Logan's paradox.

To the north, the mob surged and sections of fence collapsed. Abruptly there were men swarming inward, all along the periphery. Most of them scattered into smaller groups and milled around here and there, uncertainly. Many of them seemed surprised that they were on this side of the fence.

And a few of them ran amok. Logan grimaced as he saw a thrown brick glance off Johnny-O's helmet, and saw the young cop tumble down the rubble heap and into the pit. Moments passed, then the youth's head appeared.

Others had seen the fall, too. A policeman nearby ran to the edge of the pit, others following. Logan could hear the first one's voice. "Johnny, boy! You, Johnny-O! Saw you fall. Are you hurt?"

"I'm fine, Mac," the boy responded. Logan couldn't hear him as he turned away momentarily, but he heard, " . . . somethin' buried here. I need a sergeant to look at it."

Away to the north there were shouts, and new scuffling broke out. " . . . hold yer post," Mac was saying. "Be done here soon." The cops around the pit hurried away, and Logan saw Johnny-O starting toward the far wall of the pit.

Then, just above the pit, an anomaly swirled and coalesced, and a man in dark uniform materialized there, falling.

For the first time, Logan realized the truth of the adage, "The last thing you want to do in time-jumping is meet yourself somewhere." It was an eerie, unpleasant feeling, seeing himself materialize fifty yards away. There was an unreal, vertiginous sensation about it, like the impossible and the undeniable suddenly becoming one. Logan clenched his jaws and looked away . . . and saw something else. A little to his left, a young woman crouched behind a gravel pile. She wore postflapper attire—a severe, almost ankle-length flowered dress with rose hues that matched the huge, floppy purse she carried. A wide, ornamented hat hid her piled dark hair and her pixie face, but he knew her. Kaki Boyer—just as she had been. She was looking back the way she had come, back toward that same fence-break that Logan had used.

In the pit, he saw his earlier self turn toward the girl, and he saw Johnny-O's nightstick descend. The girl turned and edged around the gravel heap as the two in the pit fell from sight.

Logan tensed himself, watching from the shed roof. Any moment now . . .

As if on cue, the girl left the cover of the stone pile and started toward the pit, and Johnny-O—muddy and disheveled—climbed into sight. He turned toward a blue squad hurrying northward, then caught sight of the girl just as she saw him.

"Here, girl!" the cop shouted. "Where do you think you're—"

But she was already running. As Johnny-O scrambled after her she dodged through the flimsy High Steel barricade with its dire warning signs, heading directly into the dead zone.

Logan braced himself, leapt from the shack roof, and sprinted toward the barricade, angling to intercept. Patrolman John O'Hara—Johnny-O—never saw him coming.

The fleeing girl was already in the dead zone when Johnny-O broke through the barricade, his warning shouts drowned by the roar of torches, ring of hammers, and clatter of falling debris above. With a final burst of speed, Logan overtook him and tackled him from behind. As the cop fell, Logan rapped him across the temple, then dragged him back to the fence.

He was starting to pull the cop through the barricade when the air above him swirled, coalesced, and none other than Captain Eugene Matuzek sprawled across his bowed back, knocking both of them flat.

Matuzek, on top, was on his feet first. "What the hell's going on, Logan?" he demanded.

"I'll tell you about it later, Gene." Logan grinned. "Right now I need a lift home."

Epilogue

It was a stunned group that gathered in the briefing room, all of them staring in disbelief at Jack Logan.

"You changed history?" Eugene Matuzek growled. "You intentionally changed history?"

"I didn't change it," Logan drawled, leaning back in the star-witness seat. "I just rejoined it. I remembered something I'd heard when I was a kid, a sort of family secret that nobody talked about, and then when I got to thinking about what Stella Raines—the other Stella Raines—" He glanced across the table at the pale, stunned face of TEC Academy's chief hand-to-hand combat instructor, who had been summoned to this de-briefing at his demand. "—the Stella Ilyanova Raines of that other history, what she said about alternate realities being parallel time lines—and about the way her life was dominated by her grandfather—well, it all came back to me. It made sense, and nothing else did.

"Officer John O'Hara was my great-grandfather. My

241

real great-grandfather, not the one who gave my grand-father his name. I heard the rumor when I was just a kid, about how my great-grandmother 'had a little fling' before she was married, back in the thirties, and how she was al-ready 'in a family way' as they used to say, when she met and married Great-grandpa Logan. The child's real father, a New York cop, had died in a shoot-out, in some kind of ethnic riot on New York's waterfront. Great-grandpa Lo-gan knew it, of course, and he accepted my granddad as his own.

"But he wasn't. He was Johnny-O O'Hara's offspring. The same rookie cop I encountered on my launch to 1930. The one who died in that steel fall because I was there with him in that pit. Kaki Boyer would have seen him other-wise, and avoided him, and he wouldn't have been killed."

Around him, TEC debriefers sighed, shook their heads; Dale Easter cleaned his glasses; and Claire Hemmings frowned, all of them trying to sort their way through the complexities of it.

"Okay," Dale Easter breathed, finally, putting his glasses back on his nose. "So what was the ripple that sent you back there in the first place? It's gone now. What did we send you to fix? Was it Kaki Boyer's presence, a paradox creating an anachronism? . . ."

"Pretty good analogy for an anomaly," Bob O'Donnelly muttered, grinning.

"Shut up, Bob." Dale scowled in concentration. "Or was it the gold coins that Johnny-O found, and she dug up? Or what?"

Logan rubbed his eyes. Even he was becoming con-fused, and it was his recitation. "I don't think it was any of that," he said. "I think it was ChronComp itself, protecting its own existence—or, more precisely, protecting E-warp. Did you know that ChronComp has a basic fail-safe in its program . . . that it's programmed to protect its own components, even from TEC? You might want to have S and R look into that, Gene, but for God's sake don't let them delete it. It's important."

The TEC captain closed his eyes and waved a hand in front of his face, like a person besieged by mosquitos. "Protecting E-warp? The Dome system? From what?"

"From never having existed," Logan said. "E-warp was discovered by a team of NSA researchers in 1971. Nobody knew what it was until time travel came along, but they knew about it. Jimmy Sheffield was one of those researchers. Jimmy Sheffield was also Kaki Boyer's son. I think Kaki Boyer would have been killed in that construction dead zone in 1930, if I hadn't stopped Johnny-O when I did. I think she hesitated, maybe, when he wasn't behind her, and the debris that hit her only bruised her arm."

Claire Hemmings was tapping furiously at her keyboard, trying to chart the sequence of events. "But if you hadn't been there—the first you, I mean—then he wouldn't have run after her in the first place. I mean—well . . ."

Captain Matuzek slapped the briefing table with both palms. "I've lost track! God almighty!"

"Yeah," Easter mused. "He might be able to sort it out. I'm not sure we can."

"A paradox within a puzzle surrounded by a riddle," O'Donnelly quipped. "That's what happens when people have time on their hands. We're going to have to be careful with ChronComp on this one. If we start feeding in scenarios of a parallel history involving a separate, undocumented time-travel operation, we don't know what sort of fail-safes that might set off. We don't want a paranoid computer on our hands."

Across from Logan, Stella Raines was staring into space, her blue eyes far away. "An ethnic riot on the waterfront," she said, to nobody in particular. "Yes, it fits. My grandfather was badly wounded in an event like that. He was a White Russian sympathizer, part of a group protesting some U.S.-Soviet treaty. He was shot by a policeman . . . accidentally, I guess. The policeman could have been John O'Hara."

"Your grandfather?" Logan urged. "Alex Porter?"

"His real name was Aleksei Portenov. After he was wounded, he sort of lost interest in politics. He was one of the founders of Am-Can Research, but only as an investor. He died a long time ago, in a train wreck. But I have something of his that I've always carried. Kind of like a token." She opened the collar of her tunic and pulled out a medallion. "It's a remembrance, from when I was a little girl."

It was an old, golden coin.

"Part of a collection," Stella said. "He bought it from some Americans, back in the thirties."

It would all go to ChronComp . . . very carefully. It would be sorted out—or at least sanitized—or not.

So many variables, so many imponderables—multiple cross connections among events on each time line, and two distinct time lines! Maybe with enough input, ChronComp could make sense of it all, and then maybe they would all learn something they hadn't known before—just how intricate the weave of eventuality could be.

At any rate, the mission was history now and there was other work to do.

Logan was heading for the aid station to get a variety of cuts and bruises attended when Dale Easter caught up with him. The chief historian was carrying a huge book—a library volume of old newspaper copies.

"You certainly choose interesting ways to get a message through, Logan," he said. "I thought you might want to see this."

He led the way to a service counter and opened the book, thumbing through its pages. When he found what he wanted, he turned the book around for Logan. "Here," he said.

It was a page of *The New York Times*, dated in May 1930. There was a story about a labor riot in Lower Manhattan, and a photograph—an old halftone of a mob pressing in on a fenced lot while policemen confronted them. Beyond the mob, on a partly whitewashed brick wall, was a message painted in large, white letters:

TEC—NEED A LIFT HOME—LOGAN

"It worked," Logan pointed out.

"Yeah, but . . . well, graffiti?" Easter grinned at the timecop. "Nice going, Logan. Real high-tech."

*Look for these thrilling time-travel novels
by DAN PARKINSON*

THE WHISPERS
Book One of *The Gates of Time*

Time-travelers intent on discovering the origin of
Time set up a time-travel agency in a suburban
midwest home in *our* time. Rogue time-travelers,
future time-travelers, new time-travelers, reluctant
time-travelers, and one whose life is actually running backward converge on the house of one
ordinary couple . . . whose lives will never be the
same again.

FACES OF INFINITY
Book Two of *The Gates of Time*

The second novel in this series throws the retired
Kansas farm couple and their futuristic friends
into the path of a megalomaniacal genius out to
destroy all time-travel technology as a means of
becoming the King of Time.

✎ FREE DRINKS ✎

Take the Del Rey® survey and get a free newsletter! Answer the questions below and we will send you complimentary copies of the DRINK (Del Rey® Ink) newsletter free for one year. Here's where you will find out all about upcoming books, read articles by top authors, artists, and editors, and get the inside scoop on your favorite books.

Age _____ Sex ❑ M ❑ F

Highest education level: ❑ high school ❑ college ❑ graduate degree

Annual income: ❑ $0-30,000 ❑ $30,001-60,000 ❑ over $60,000

Number of books you read per month: ❑ 0-2 ❑ 3-5 ❑ 6 or more

Preference: ❑ fantasy ❑ science fiction ❑ horror ❑ other fiction ❑ nonfiction

I buy books in hardcover: ❑ frequently ❑ sometimes ❑ rarely

I buy books at: ❑ superstores ❑ mall bookstores ❑ independent bookstores
❑ mail order

I read books by new authors: ❑ frequently ❑ sometimes ❑ rarely

I read comic books: ❑ frequently ❑ sometimes ❑ rarely

I watch the Sci-Fi cable TV channel: ❑ frequently ❑ sometimes ❑ rarely

I am interested in collector editions (signed by the author or illustrated):
❑ yes ❑ no ❑ maybe

I read Star Wars novels: ❑ frequently ❑ sometimes ❑ rarely

I read Star Trek novels: ❑ frequently ❑ sometimes ❑ rarely

I read the following newspapers and magazines:

❑ *Analog*	❑ *Locus*	❑ *Popular Science*
❑ *Asimov*	❑ *Wired*	❑ *USA Today*
❑ *SF Universe*	❑ *Realms of Fantasy*	❑ *The New York Times*

Check the box if you do not want your name and address shared with qualified vendors ❑

Name _____
Address _____
City/State/Zip _____
E-mail _____

timecop

PLEASE SEND TO: DEL REY®/The DRINK
201 EAST 50TH STREET, NEW YORK, NY 10022 OR FAX TO
THE ATTENTION OF DEL REY PUBLICITY 212/572-2676